TEMPTED BY A LADY'S SMILE

TEMPTED BY A LADY'S SMILE

Christi Caldwell

For more information about the author:
christicaldwellauthor@gmail.com
www.christicaldwellauthor.com

ISBN: 1944240209
ISBN-13: 9781944240202

DEDICATION

To Doug: a loving father, an amazing husband, and my best
friend. Through appointments, specialists, school meetings, and
everything in-between, you are there at our side. Thank you for
encouraging me, and allowing me, every day to fulfill my dream.
You are my real-life hero. (And a pretty wonderful cook, too!)

ONE

Somerset, England
Summer 1821

Miss Gemma Reed was neither pretty nor talented.

As a young girl she'd attributed her nursemaid's lamentations to, well, *meanness*. At eight and ten years of age when Gemma had made her Come Out, however, the finding had been unequivocally handed down by the *ton*.

She was ugly.

Or, that is what had been decided and written with regular frequency by Polite Society during her first Season. Now, three Seasons later, the verdict had proven the same. It was all the more bothersome when a young lady was saddled with a name like Gemma, when she was the farthest thing from a Diamond. As the papers had so cleverly, or rather, *un*-cleverly, pointed out.

Gemma wrinkled her nose. In *her* estimation, ugly was quite harsh.

The carriage hit a large bump on the old Roman road leading to Somerset and her copy of Georges Cuvier's *Le Règne Animal* tumbled to the floor. Gemma winced and bent to retrieve it.

She sat up just as her brother's black barouche bounced once more. With a sigh Gemma abandoned her reading and put aside the small tome. *Blasted carriage ride.* She discreetly rubbed the spot just above her derrière.

Mother glanced over and frowned. "Do stop touching yourself. It is impolite." Before Gemma could formulate a reply to that admonishment, her mother tipped her chin at the leather volume on the bench.

1

"And be certain to have that hidden before we arrive. It won't do to be seen carrying around a medical story."

"It is a science journal," she muttered, earning another reproachful look from her mama. As her disapproving mama launched into a lecture about appropriate reading material for a young lady, Gemma peeled back the gold curtain and stared at the passing countryside.

No, she'd never be considered conventional *or* pretty.

And though she didn't quite see herself as a raving beauty nor even remotely beautiful, neither did she think she was the *horribly* unattractive figure painted by the *ton*. The talented part, well, that particular insult she would have to agree with them, on, however. That is, talents as they pertained to ladylike ventures—needlepoint, singing, fluttering a fan, watercolors. All endeavors she was rubbish at. And that was being generous. Yes, by Society's standards she was neither pretty nor graceful and certainly not talented. With the exception of archery, the talents she did possess would never be seen as appropriate, proper, and as such, would never be remarked on by the *ton*. She could ride, shoot, and hold an archer's bow better than the most skilled gentleman. Such a feat would never earn a lady any attention that was good and it would, most assuredly, not land her a husband.

The carriage hit another jarring bump and Gemma slammed against the side of the conveyance. "Bloody hell!" The curse slipped out and then she promptly bit the inside of her cheek.

"Gemma," Mama scolded, giving her head a disapproving shake. "Do be sure to not speak so in front of His Grace, or the duke's son, or..."

As her mother proceeded through the list of the distinguished guests who would be attending the Duke of Somerset's summer party, Gemma redirected her attention out the window. Being the only friend to Lady Beatrice Dennington, the daughter of their host, Gemma well knew who would be in attendance and the very specific reason for this grand summer party. She and the young lady had struck up an unlikely friendship; both on their fourth Seasons and both unwed, except Beatrice was a glorious beauty while Gemma was...well, *Gemma.*

Propping her chin on her hand, she stared longingly out at the rolling green hills and the passing countryside.

Just then, her brother, Emery, Viscount Smithfield, brought his horse alongside the carriage. She eyed his mount with a vicious hungering and her legs twitched with the need for being astride her own horse. She closed her eyes a long moment and imagined racing through the sprawling land with the wind in her face, free of Society's snide comments, free of her mother's chastisement, free of all of it. Gemma opened her eyes. Alas, ladies did not ride astride. They sat dutifully in carriages with tedium threatening to be the death of them and dreamed of a grand romance with their best friend's brother. Her gaze collided with Emery. He gave her a knowing half-grin and a wink. A grin and a wink that said he well knew her love for riding and knew she belonged out there with him…if the world was an altogether different place for polite ladies.

Gemma let the curtain go and it fluttered back into place, swallowing the view of crisp, blue, summer skies and fluffy, white clouds and she, in this moment, felt not unlike a gilded bird trapped in a cage.

"…There are rumors that the marquess will wed Lady Diana," her mother's lamentations pulled her back to the moment. Her discourse brought every conversation, as it invariably did, back 'round to the talk of husbands.

The muscles of her stomach clenched. There was no doubt just which marquess her mother referred to. All the *ton* spoke of or cared about was the gentleman's rank and wealth. And it was well known about town that the Duke of Somerset was suffering a wasting illness and this summer event had been designed and carefully arranged with the specific purpose of seeing his unwed daughter, Lady Beatrice, *also* approaching her fourth Season, as well as his son, Robert, the Marquess of Westfield, married.

"But I say if the son's match was already determined, then the duke would not be hosting this summer party."

Gemma resisted the urge to jam her fingertips against her temples and rub the growing ache caused by her mother's prattling. As her grasping parent continued on about the marquess' marital prospects,

Gemma again yanked back the curtain and stared intently out the lead window.

The ladies invited to attend the duke's summer party would all do so with the intent purpose of making a match—ideally with the Marquess of Westfield. Tall, broad-shouldered, and ruggedly handsome, he was a glorious specimen of masculine perfection...and a smidge below royalty, given his future title, every lady's not so secret wish in her bridegroom.

And Gemma didn't give a jot about any of it—his wealth, his male beauty, his title of marquess and eventual duke. She'd been in love with the man for three years now. Since her partnerless first Season, when he'd offered her a quadrille on the disastrous day of her Come Out. Oh, she wasn't so naïve that she'd give a man her heart for one small, though heroic, act. He'd been the only gentleman to partner her in a set at whatever event he was in attendance. Never two dances together to signify anything more, but those single dances mattered to her.

"...Tell me you will have a care at the duke's party."

Silence registered and, blinking several times, Gemma shifted her attention from the passing countryside to her mother. With her perfect golden curls and sapphire blue eyes, could not a single speck of that beauty have passed to Gemma? Not that she minded being...well, plain, it was just that...

"Well?" Mama prodded, favoring Gemma with an entreating look.

Her mind raced. What were they speaking on? Ah, right. In a roundabout way, Mama was pleading with her to watch her tongue and avoid embarrassment. "I promise to be nothing but myself," she pledged.

That, thankfully, led to an endless speech on the perils in Gemma attending the most coveted summer event. She'd long been an oddity in her own family. Emery, with his blond locks and captivating demeanor, charmed young ladies and dowagers alike. Her flawlessly beautiful mother was a leading hostess and matron. And then there was Gemma; who was everything...well, *ordinary*. Limp, brown hair that could not curl with a prayer and a magical brush. Plain brown eyes. Not even the type of brown with flecks of gold or green in them. Just brown. At five feet four inches, she was not too tall, not too short.

She startled as a hand touched her knee and she lifted her gaze.

Her mother gave her a gentle look. "There is no reason you cannot make a match with the marquess." The softly spoken words were said with a mother's pride and love.

She mustered a smile. "I know," she replied automatically. There was no *one* reason. Rather, there were all number of reasons she couldn't.

Mama leaned closer. "Even if it is not the marquess, you will find the gentleman who will appreciate you and love you for who you are."

What her mother could not know was that Gemma had already found the gentleman she would spend her days with. For now, she loved him and appreciated him, and it was merely a matter of bringing the gentleman around to the truth that all of those quadrilles, waltzes, and reels were more than mere polite dances.

The carriage rumbled down a drive, on through the park-like grounds of an opulent estate. Fountains lined the graveled drive; the stone adornments at odds with the tucked away corner of Somerset owned by the duke.

They had arrived.

Gemma's heart pounded hard and fast, and where her mother's ramblings had previously aggravated, now she welcomed the distracted prattling about proper summer party etiquette. Welcomed the diversion away from the very sudden realness of her planned meeting with Lord Westfield where she would, at last, confess all that was in her heart to him.

And what had *seemed* so very simple, now seemed the manner of failed tasks assigned laughingly by the gods to watch a mere mortal fail.

I cannot...

As soon as the cowardly thought slid in, Gemma firmed her jaw. Failure was not an option. For if she didn't, at the very least, confess her feelings to Lord Westfield then she would forever harbor regret of what might have been and what should have been, if she'd not been

5

a coward. Yes, she'd been labeled unattractive, ungainly, and untalented, in her two and twenty years, but not once had she been called a coward.

The carriage dipped as their driver climbed from the box. A moment later, the door was pulled open and the liveried servant held a hand out to assist the viscountess from the carriage.

Relishing the momentary quiet, Gemma collected her book and then reluctantly placed her fingers in the young man's hand. She offered him a smile. "Thank you, Connor."

He inclined his head. "Miss Reed."

Gemma's feet settled on the ground and she moved her legs experimentally, willing movement back into them after countless hours of uninterrupted sitting. She placed one hand on the small of her back and arched—

"Never let Mother see you doing something as scandalous as stretching."

At the unexpected drawl, Gemma spun and promptly lost her balance. Her small, leather tome fell indignantly to the earth.

Emery shot his hands out and steadied her at the shoulders.

"Gemma," Mother called.

Their mother missed nothing. Why, she could be used to ferret out secrets for the Home Office with the eyes she possessed.

Emery retrieved Gemma's book and handed it over. "I told you," he whispered.

She laughed, tucking Cuvier's work under her arm. "Yes, well, she does value propriety." As such, she'd long despaired of Gemma's penchant for garnering all the wrong kinds of notice.

"And good matches," Emery put in with a wink. He offered his elbow and Gemma slid her fingers onto his sleeve.

"I daresay you are the real reason for her hopes with this event," she said out the side of her mouth.

Alas, poor Emery had been dodging their mother's clear attempts to make a match for him since he'd left university nearly eight years ago. She'd been less than veiled in her aspirations for him to make a match with the still unwed Lady Beatrice.

As they climbed the stairs of the palatial estate, the butler threw the doors wide. With Emery at her side, Gemma hesitated. *Do not be a coward...*Drawing in a steadying breath, she forced her feet into a forward movement.

"You look as pained as I about being here," Emery whispered as they were ushered through the long, carpeted corridors to their respective guest rooms.

"What would I have to be pained about?" she shot back, waggling her eyebrows. "My mother's pathetic attempt at matchmaking? Or her desperate wish to see me wed any suitable gentleman before the London Season begins?"

Their melded laughter earned a frown from their mother and Gemma tamped down her smile. They made their way through the labyrinth that was the Duke of Somerset's country estate and Gemma peeked about. It was hard *not* to gape at the evidence of such opulent wealth. Elaborate gilt frames hung upon the satin-wallpapered walls with stern, disapproving ducal ancestors looking on at Gemma.

She drew her book close to her chest. Or mayhap it was her reading material they disapproved of.

Regardless, even those long-dead ancestors no doubt recognized a flawed lady amidst their ghostly midst.

How many of the guests now occupying these hallowed walls coveted the lavish adornments? And yet, the ornate, gold sconces lining the halls and the mahogany furniture artfully placed throughout the abode made Gemma's hands moist. And not in the greedy, grasping way of the ladies who now darted their gazes about did, but with the panicky, nausea-inducing dread that came from being an out-of-place oddity amidst this elaborate household.

She wrinkled her nose. Why did Lord Westfield have to be a future duke? Why couldn't he be a baron, or knight, or even a successful merchant? All of those would do a good deal more preferable than falling in love with the gentleman whose future title commanded awe, power, and respect just by being uttered.

"You are not usually this quiet," Emery observed.

"I gathered Mama had enough to say for the whole of the family."

A sharp laugh escaped Emery and she welcomed that calming, familiar chuckle as it echoed off the hallway walls. The sound of it made the Duke of Somerset's estate more of a home and less of a... tomb. Yes, it would have been far preferable if Lord Westfield had proven a lesser lord and not a gentleman on the cusp of inheriting a near kingdom.

A short while later, Gemma was shown to her room, while her family continued on to their respective chambers. With blessed silence her only company, she tossed her copy of *Le Règne Animal* onto a nearby table, and then layered her back against the paneled door. She closed her eyes.

She'd thought overly long about finding the gumption to confess her feelings to Lord Westfield and, yet, now that she was here, she'd really not considered how one went about finding a gentleman amidst a crowded house party—or rather, finding a gentleman *alone*.

Knock Knock Knock

A gasp burst from Gemma's lips and she jumped. Pressing a hand to her chest, she pulled the door open, and her only friend in the world, Lady Beatrice Dennington spilled inside.

"Oh, thank goodness, you've arrived." The perfectly golden-haired young lady flung her arms about Gemma. She staggered back a step, before returning the embrace.

In an instant, she took in the tight drawn lines at the corner of Beatrice's mouth and the glimmer of sadness in her cerulean blue eyes. A pang struck Gemma over her own selfishness. She captured Beatrice's hands and gave a slight squeeze. "How are you?" she asked softly. The same way the *ton* saw in Gemma an unattractive bluestocking, undeserving of notice, was not unlike the way in which they viewed the flawlessly perfect, blonde-haired, blue-eyed beauty. They failed to see the young woman Beatrice truly was, hoping for love, and even now suffering a broken heart over her father's slow death.

Beatrice's lips formed a brittle, forced smile. "Fine," she said. "I am fine. Truly," she added. The muscles of her throat moved and then she returned Gemma's squeeze. "Enough with that. Let us focus on this horrid event my father has organized." Yes, it was far safer to speak on those proper affairs, than in death, dying, and inevitable loss. "It's been dreadfully dull without you. Countless guests simpering over Robert and gentlemen feigning an interest in me." She mumbled that last part, high color filling her cheeks. "As though they seek anything more than a ducal connection and the wealth attached to my name."

Gemma snorted. "It could be a good deal worse. You could have no gentlemen showing any interest whatsoever in you."

"I would prefer that," Beatrice said matter-of-factly. Taking Gemma by the hand, she guided her purposefully toward the bed. "Better than to be courted and then passed over again and again and again and again." Which Society well knew to be the case for Beatrice, who'd been courted by no fewer than three gentlemen who'd all gone on to wed another. Gemma would never figure out just what it was a gentleman wanted in a lady when he'd pass over one such as Beatrice. "I've no intention of making a match with someone desiring my dowry." Beatrice shoved her into a sit.

Gemma bounced on the soft mattress wrinkling the smooth, satin coverlet.

"Enough of me." A determined glint lit Beatrice's eyes that would have terrified a battle-hardened soldier. "We are discussing you."

Gemma blinked. "We are?"

"We are," Beatrice confirmed with an emphatic nod. "That is, your marital prospects."

"I don't have any prospects." She merely had a hope and a prayer for the most sought-after, lord in the realm. A hope and a prayer, indeed.

Beatrice cast a look over at the closed door and then quickly claimed the spot beside Gemma. "And I've no doubt, Robert sees how truly special you are," her loyal friend went on.

"Yes, but he must see me...amidst all the other ladies in attendance." In short, a wilted weed among vibrant, fragrant, summer blooms. With a drawn out sigh, Gemma flopped backward on the bed. She stared at the broad, floral canopy overhead. What sorry days, indeed, when one relied on the aid of one's friend to bring a gentleman up to scratch.

9

The mattress dipped as Beatrice lay beside her, shoulder to shoulder. "The man you've set your sights on is unlike the others. He sees past the preening and the fawning."

Yes, Beatrice should know. After all, the gentleman in question was, in fact, her brother.

Her friend turned her head and gave a conspiratorial smile. "Furthermore, you have something the other ladies in attendance do not."

"Oh, and what is that?" Gemma looked expectantly back at her.

"Why, you have me to help." Beatrice popped up. "Robert is now fishing at the lake and should return near dusk, prior to the dinner party." Beatrice stared pointedly at her. "Ahem."

Gemma pushed herself into a sitting position alongside her friend. Why was Beatrice looking at her in that way? She shook her head once.

"I said ahem," Beatrice made another clearing sound with her throat. "Robert." She nudged her in the side. "He will be fishing at the lake at the edge of Papa's property."

Fishing at dusk. A soft sigh slipped past her lips. Of course the marquess would be clever enough to see the benefit in casting his line at that hour. Though in truth…Gemma chewed at her lower lip. "It is a *nearly* perfect idea," she conceded.

Her friend's smile dipped. "*Nearly* perfect?"

Oh, indeed. "Yes, well, during the day is an atrocious time because a fish has unlimited visibility. Ideally, dusk and just after dusk would be preferable given the angle of the ultraviolet light through the angles of—"

"Gemma." Taking her by the shoulders, Beatrice looked her in the eye. "I am *not* discussing Robert's cleverness in the sport of fishing."

She tipped her head. "You aren't?" Then what had been the whole point of mentioning his early evening excursion?

"No. I wasn't." Beatrice closed her eyes and her lips moved as though in prayer. She opened her eyes. "I am telling you he'll be at the lake." The other lady gave her a pointed look. "Fishing." When Gemma still said nothing, her friend tossed her hands up. "Alone. He will be alone."

As her friend's meaning became at last clear, Gemma widened her eyes. A strangled laugh escaped her. "Surely you do not expect—?"

The mischievous glimmer that lit the flawless Lady Beatrice's eyes would have shocked the *ton*. "I do expect it. Why, you know Robert is a rogue, so he needs a bit of a *push* and you are the one to give him that push." She waggled her blonde eyebrows. "With a bit of assistance from your dearest friend."

Her dearest and only friend. Regardless, she'd come to appreciate there was more good in having a loving, loyal friend like Beatrice than a ballroom full of false figures who didn't know or care about her interests.

Gemma returned her attention to the canopy overhead. If her mother could hear her scheming, she would scuttle her off to London. After all, with her penchant for finding trouble, such plans could only end one way…

Now she must hope that one way involved marriage to Robert, the Marquess of Westfield.

TWO

A summer party thrown together with the sole intention of matchmaking the respective guests in attendance was one Mr. Richard Jonas would typically avoid at all costs.

At three and thirty years, with the recently acquired reputation of rogue, and a desire to live for his own pleasures, the last thing he had any interest in was marriage. With the prospect of his own family gathering in the Kent countryside, he'd picked the far lesser of the two evils and accepted the invite of his childhood friend, Lord Westfield, and future Duke of Somerset.

Richard withdrew a flask from his pocket and took a swill of brandy, surveying the country lake. The dark blue sky dusted in crimson and orange ushered in night and cast a glow upon the smooth water.

Then, avoiding his family and the prospect of marriage hadn't always been the case for Richard. Once, he'd desired marriage and… *more*, with a certain young woman.

Richard grimaced and took another swill. Said woman who happened to now be his sister-in-law, Lady Eloise, now blissfully and quite lovingly wedded to his younger brother. Yes, when presented with the possibility of seeing his very happily wed, now-expecting sister-in-law and his brother, he chose to face the ladies bent on matchmaking. Not that he had a care where those young women were concerned. After all, a viscount's younger brother stood little chance of inheriting and offered little by way of a title or match for a grasping lady.

Only one woman he'd known had never been grasping. A gentle summer breeze stirred ripples upon the otherwise placid lake and he swirled the contents of his flask. Nay, Eloise hadn't cared a jot for titles or wealth, as was demonstrated by her unwavering love of his title-less brother, Lucien. Lucien, who'd languished in a hospital for years, offered no title, had lost an arm to infection from a war wound, and served as a butler to some powerful lord. And none of that had mattered to Eloise. He put the stopper back on his flask. Just as Richard had never truly mattered to her. Not in the ways he'd most wanted to matter.

Unbidden, his gaze went to the fishing reel, as buried memories slipped to the surface of the only girl he'd ever known who'd baited a hook. His lips twitched with wry mirth. A young girl who'd baited the hook of his then squeamish self and who'd never laughed about that weakness. Even when his own brothers had mocked and jeered as only brothers could.

Tucking his drink inside his front pocket, Richard retrieved his pole and carried it to the edge of the shore.

"Do you intend to remain out here through dinner?" Amusement lingered in the question from his companion.

Richard glanced back to where Lord Westfield knelt gathering his fishing equipment and then returned his stare to the lake. "Indeed." He cast his line.

Behind him, Westfield's mutterings reached his ears. "Some of us are not afforded that same luxury."

No, there were certain expectations and responsibilities that went with his birthright.

Where most begrudged the other man for his possession of an eventual dukedom, Richard had never wanted, craved, or envied the other man the responsibilities and headaches which came with his title. Sought after by every marriage-minded miss in the realm, Westfield was not afforded the same peace that came from being a spare to the heir.

In a bid to be helpful, Richard said, "It is just a week." They both knew how endless a week would be when a duke threw together a guest list of possible matches for his two unwed children.

Westfield snorted. "The highlight of each night will be when this is over and I'm free to escape from the machinations of those present."

Yes, all who knew of or about the marquess were aware of the time he spent at his clubs. Matchmaking summer parties and tedious respectable events were not the manner of *pleasures* he'd ever enjoyed. "You are certain you don't care to join me?" his friend asked, interrupting his thoughts.

Richard shot another look over his shoulder. The other man stood with his pole tucked on his shoulder. He shook his head. "I'll join you for drinks and not much more than that." The official events organized for the ducal party commenced on the morn, at which point Richard would do his due diligence as a guest and take part in the painful inanities.

"Brandies, then," Westfield conceded. "You're—"

"I'm certain," he interrupted dryly not bothering to turn around.

Muttering under his breath, Westfield's feet crushed the brush and gravel as he made his way to his Friesian, one of the finest mounts Richard had bred in the course of his career.

Moments later, the other man galloped off and Richard was left with his own thoughts. Of course, he'd have to join the festivities. He'd come here, after all, with the express intention of avoiding his own family's summer party.

His line pulled and Richard gave his pole a swift and strong jerk backward and up. He pumped and lifted the rod from the water while drawing in the line. The fish at the other end tugged and Richard engaged in a gentle dance, luring the creature forward as it twisted and spiraled at the end of the hook.

Richard carefully withdrew the metal from the trout's mouth and the slippery creature slid from his fingers. It turned and gyrated upon the earth, seeking escape. He eyed it a moment. How very much alike he was to that creature. Taking pity on it, he bent and rescued the trout. Carrying it to the edge of the shore, he set it in the lake, allowing the fish its freedom. Richard stared after the trout until it disappeared. The world of Polite Society was one Richard had never belonged to. The *ton* had limited interest or uses for a second-born son, just as Richard himself had little desire to be fully immersed in that world, beyond the business connections he might form as a horse breeder.

His friendship, in and of itself, with the future Duke of Somerset was all the more remarkable for it. One gentleman, so wholly born to belong in that world, and the other, embracing any chance to be free of it.

One of the most successful horse breeders in England with a small parcel of land left him by his father, Richard despised rubbing elbows with the peerage of which he was only loosely a member. His infrequent attendance at *ton* events was for no other reason than building his business. It had never been about making a match, but rather about adding clients to his already impressive list.

Richard gathered his belongings and then strode over to his packs. He clicked his tongue twice and his mount trotted over. He reluctantly swung his leg over Warrior's broad back and then urged him on to the duke's estate. Yes, at any other moment, in any other time, he would readily say the Duke of Somerset's summer matchmaking party was the last place he cared to be.

That was until Eloise had broken his heart. Now he cared to be wherever that young woman was not. Even with the peerage.

Leaning over his mount's withers, he gave him room to stretch his legs and the obedient creature flew. As he put distance between him and the lake, he guided Warrior onward toward the opulent residence. Richard reveled in the clean summer air slapping at his face, embraced the feel of it as it whipped his hair. This was the world he truly belonged to; on the fringe of Society, in the countryside without anyone in his—

A small figure in soft yellow skirts stood transfixed ten paces away, gawking and gaping like that just restored trout from moments ago.

Richard let fly a black curse and quickly pulled on the reins and the young woman stumbled back, tripping over her skirts in her haste to back away. With a loud whinny, Warrior pawed and scratched at the air, before settling onto the earth in a flurry of gravel and dust. Heart pounding, Richard leapt from his mount. What in blazes was the lady doing so far from the estate? And more, what would possess her to step into a galloping horse's path? Seething fury leant his steps an agitated movement. "Are you hurt, miss?" he bit out, stalking forward.

Coming to a quick stop, Richard towered over the young lady still in repose and he held a hand out. The quality of her satin skirts revealed her to be a guest and he gritted his teeth in annoyance at another empty-brained miss wandering the grounds in search of the ducal heir. What else accounted for her presence here even now with dinner being served in a short while? An altogether different rage gripped him. Years earlier, Westfield had his heart shattered by a grasping woman, the details of that time he no longer spoke of. Now there was an entire household of ladies circling the man like vultures about their prey.

This *particular* vulture stared unblinkingly up at him. A limp, brown tress hung over her eye.

"I asked you whether you were hurt, miss," he said between tight lips, and in the absence of an immediate reply, gripped her by her arms and settled her on her feet.

She possessed dull, brown hair, equally dull, brown eyes, and a remarkably pale visage, which he'd wager his entire line of horses, was not a product of her near fall, and more his not treating her as a cherished, treasured miss.

Her mouth fell open, and then emotion sparkled within those brown depths, making her eyes…well, not so very uninteresting. "I beg your pardon," she snapped.

"As you should for stepping out into a man's riding path at dusk."

The irises of her eyes disappeared under the narrowing of her stare. "I was most decidedly not apologizing."

"Of course you weren't." He infused a drollness into his tone that brought the lady's eyebrows shooting up.

She planted her hands on her hips. "What in blazes is *that* supposed to mean?"

As had been his experience with other ladies of quality. They'd vied for a place in his bed, a pleasure he'd forgone for his devotion to Eloise and the hope of more with that particular and uniquely different lady. But never did they apologize and always did they expect the world was their due. Having learned long ago that it was a decidedly dangerous path to travel down in terms of arguing with a woman about the merits of an apology, he inclined his head. "Forgive me, I was unprepared to see a young lady in the middle of the riding path at this late hour." Unchaperoned. He let that word go unsaid between them.

She peered intently at him as though seeking the veracity of his claim and then some of the tension left her small shoulders. "Forgive me," she returned, shocking him with that apology. "You are, indeed, correct. I wandered too far from the party and I was seeking someone out. A friend," she said on a rush when he narrowed his eyes. "A proper friend. Nothing scandalous, at all." The high-pitched timbre of her voice hinted at an altogether different tale. This mousy miss would hardly be the first lady who'd tried to orchestrate Westfield into a compromising position.

Richard folded his arms at his chest and eyed the chit with renewed wariness. "A friend?" His horse pawed at the earth. Even Warrior knew to be suspicious of this one.

"Yes. A friend." Tension dripped from the young woman's frame and she skittered her gaze about before ultimately settling it on Richard's mount.

He opened his mouth to press the suspicious miss for details when she moved closer to Warrior and scratched the creature between his eyes. Some of the tightness went out of the lady's shoulders. Warrior whinnied and leaned into that touch. Richard furrowed his brow. Well, mayhap his horse was less discriminatory than he'd thought. "What are you doing?"

The lady followed his stare. "Uh, petting your horse." She dropped her hand almost reluctantly to her side. "But y-you are correct. I should be…"

He stepped into her path, blocking her escape. At his side, Warrior danced nervously and he stroked his dampened withers until the horse calmed. "Never tell me? You were looking for a particular marquess, whose father would have him wed?" He didn't know where the desire to bait the young lady came from.

She stiffened, but the crimson blush on her cheeks confirmed his supposition. Of course. Another duke-hunter. "Do not be silly," she said with a damning weakness. "Wh-why should Lord Westfield be fishing at this hour? Hmm?" The bold chit didn't allow him a chance to respond. "He wouldn't. Granted, dusk allows the fish to see *some* of the ultraviolet spectrum, but there is still the matter of the duke's dinner party." Richard cocked his head. *Ultraviolet spectrum?* What was she on about? "And I, as a respectable young lady, would hardly be searching for him when he was returning from his outing." The lady gave a jaunty toss of her nonexistent curls. "N-nor is it your place as the duke's steward," Steward? He furrowed his brow. "To corner and chide one of his guests."

The lady chatted more than a magpie. And if she hadn't perjured herself with plans to trap his closest friend in the world, why then he'd think there was something endearing in her ability to prattle on. But she did inadvertently reveal her plans for Westfield and, as such, placed herself neatly into the category of graspers, just like every other lady ducal-heir-hunting this week.

"I didn't mention fishing."

She ceased blinking and cocked her head.

"Fishing," he said drolly. "I mentioned nothing about Westfield fishing."

The young miss in her ruffled yellow skirts opened and closed her mouth several times. "Neither did I. I *merely* said he would not be fishing and he wouldn't. Not at this hour. Even with the ultraviolet spectrum," she added once more.

Goodness, for his disgust with all the ladies who'd line themselves here and all but bare their teeth for a chance at the title of duchess, there was something to admire in this one's temerity and fearlessness. It made an otherwise plain young woman…someone rather, interesting.

The lady brushed that loose, what might or might not have been, curl behind her ear. "Regardless, it is hardly proper for me to stand here discussing Lord Westfield's whereabouts with you. Or any matter, for that matter." She wrinkled her nose at that redundancy.

Despite very nearly being thrown from his mount and the annoyance at this lady who, given the chance, would trap his friend, his lips twitched.

She flared her eyes. "Are you laughing at me?"

God, the lady didn't require a single word from him to fill an entire conversation. He opened his mouth—

"Because I assure you, the duke would not approve of your highhandedness with a young la—" Her words ended on a startled squeak as he closed the slight distance between them and, in one fluid movement, wrapped his arms about her.

All the saints in heaven, in all her penchant for finding trouble and recklessness, never in her plans to speak alone with Lord Westfield had the duke's steward or any other stranger fit into her imaginings of how this moment was to proceed.

Gemma swallowed hard and a thrill of awareness shot through her from the point of the man's touch. She should revile him. So why did warmth continue to spiral through her? It was an irrational response to this man who was nothing more than a stranger—a towering, darkhaired, broad-shouldered stranger with features too rugged to ever be considered truly beautiful. Giving her head a clearing shake, Gemma sought to put her jumbled senses to rights as the perils of being here alone, in his arms, no less, registered. She shoved against him. "Release me this instant or I shall inform the duke of your highhandedness." It was a lie. A bald-faced, obvious lie. She knew it and the wryly-grinning man before her knew it. She could no sooner admit to wandering the estates, unchaperoned, and being held in this man's arms than she could hitch up her skirts and run wild through the duke's home singing the verse of a bawdy tavern song taught her by her brother. To confess any of this would mean ruin. And yet, despite the anxiety pitting her belly, her body burned with the heat emanating from his muscular frame.

The steward drew her forward, raising her on her feet, so close their lips nearly brushed. "I do not care to be threatened, particularly by one such as you."

Her heart hammered wildly and she feared it would beat a rhythm right out of her chest. "One such as me?" She prided herself on the steady deliverance of those words.

"A tart-mouthed, prideful, arrogant, young lady."

His audacious charge rang a gasp from her. Oh, that was quite enough. Convincing herself that warmth had been as imagined as the hint of a smile she'd seen moments ago, Gemma shoved at his chest to no avail. She could no sooner move his broad-muscled frame than she could move the border of the Duke of Somerset's property. "I am not arrogant." A young lady who couldn't bring a single gentleman up to scratch for so much as a waltz didn't have much pride left to go around where men were concerned and that included the lofty nobles and the callous brutes like this one.

"Are you not?" he whispered. His gaze went to her mouth.

And for the slightest moment, she imagined he would kiss her and perhaps it was curiosity because she was now two and twenty and still never been kissed; not by a gentleman or even a too-bold village boy in her younger years. But a part of her longed to know the taste of him.

He filled his hands with her buttocks, sculpting his hands about them. She gasped. *Push him away, Gemma Reed. You are very much in love with Robert and this is the ultimate betrayal.* And yet there was nothing else for it. Gemma was an absolute wanton for she wanted his kiss, anyway.

A slow, triumphant smile curved his lips upward effectively quashing that desire borne of curiosity. She opened her mouth to blister his ears with curses when he kissed her. Gemma stiffened. She'd dreamed her first kiss would be a gentle, chaste and properly placed one by a proper gentleman. This explosion of raw vitality and passion was nothing that she could have imagined, nor anything she could have read of in any of the scandalous novels she'd devoured through the years. He continued worshiping her mouth, slanting his lips over hers again and again as though branding her as his. She moaned and he slipped his tongue inside, tasting her. And she, in turn, reveled in the taste of him. He was brandy and mint...and the faintest hint of cheroots, intoxicating and purely masculine.

He drew back and a little moan of protest bubbled in her throat. "Mayhap not arrogant, then," he whispered, brushing a kiss to where her pulse pounded hard in her neck. "Not if you'd accept the kiss of a stranger."

His damnable calm doused all the delicious butterflies dancing in her belly. In a move shown her by Emery when she'd been a young girl, Gemma jerked her knee up but the gentleman swiftly closed his long fingers about her knee. He caressed her through the fabric of her skirts setting off a delicious fluttering low in her belly. *Words, Gemma. Indignant, furious words. Say something. Anything.* "D-don't touch me. Or I shall tell the duke." She cringed. That was the very boldest retort she had after his bold, if magical, embrace? *I am a wanton.* Surely there was nothing else to explain this tumult of emotion.

"Will you?" A challenge laced that question.

"The marquess won't a-approve of your k-kissing his guests." Gemma yanked her knee free of his hold. That abrupt movement sent her tipping back and she tossed her arms out to keep from toppling over in an undignified heap, but he shot a hand out and easily steadied her.

"Won't he, love?" He wrapped that last word in a husky, slightly mocking endearment.

"You wouldn't understand, sir, because you clearly are not a gentleman." She settled her hands upon her hips.

"I imagine he'll have more questions about why a supposed lady is wandering his property with no proper chaperone."

At the unerring truth and accuracy to that charge, a dull flush heated her entire body and she tripped over herself in her bid to get away. And hating that this man was accurate and hating how very damning this seemed to him in his opinion of her attempts at "trapping" the marquess and her scandalous return of his kiss.

Given his position on the estates, however, there was little need for their paths to again cross. Which was, indeed, good. "If you will excuse me?" she asked stiffly. Not allowing him a chance to respond, she spun on her heel and sprinted down the graveled path, on to the entrance of the Duke of Somerset's grand home.

The back of her neck burned from the eyes trained on her by the gruff, mannerless, towering steward. The quality of his attire revealed him to be a member of the duke's staff and yet he spoke in the cultured tones with the insolent charges of a man of loftier origins. The quality of his horseflesh also revealed him to be a man of some wealth.

And whoever the stranger had been...he'd discovered her, which would prove calamitous to her intentions for this entire blasted event—to bring Lord Westfield 'round. Being caught alone, with her hair tumbled past her shoulders, and racing in such an indecorous manner would cause nothing less than a scandal. Then, mayhap the stranger didn't truly find anything of interest in her gallivanting about the grounds—alone. She stole a quick look over her shoulder and even with the distance she'd placed between them, found his eyes burning into the path she now traveled. Gemma hurriedly yanked her stare forward.

Her breath coming fast from her exertions, Gemma skidded to a halt outside the rear entrance of the palatial estate. She brushed her hands over her flushed cheeks and then stood frozen until she regained a semblance of calm. Shoving aside thoughts of the duke's steward, she returned her attention to what, rather who, was responsible for her having been traipsing about the lake.

Her first efforts at locating Lord Westfield had proven wholly dismal. Gemma firmed her jaw. For all Society had to say about her, there was one elemental piece they'd not gleaned—she was a determined young lady.

And she was determined to capture the Marquess of Westfield's heart.

THREE

I n the course of his thirty-three years, Richard had never been one of those gentlemen who'd caroused, wagered, and drank.

Until just recently, that was. Much had changed—as was evidenced by the brandy even now in his hand and the thick plume of smoke from his previously lit cheroot.

Since Eloise had married his younger brother...if one wanted to be truly precise. Now Richard quite enjoyed a good bottle of spirits and a turn at the gaming tables.

In addition to drinking and wagering, it would seem he had *also* become the manner of man who say...taunted blushing young ladies and sent them fleeing in fright, and only after he'd kissed them sense-less. His body stirred with the memory of the nameless schemer. Not a lady who'd ever be considered classically beautiful, or even really remotely pretty, that particular figure had occupied his thoughts since he'd returned to the duke's estate.

"How many points?"

Richard swirled the contents of his drink as Westfield's inquiry cut across his musings. Thrusting aside the memory of the young woman, Richard returned his focus to the billiards game. "Five hundred?"

Westfield snorted. "You've no intention of leaving this room, then?"

"I expect with the number of ladies seeking to corner and trap you, that would be preferable." A garrulous miss with limp, brown hair flitted to his mind.

A muscle jumped at the corner of Westfield's eye. "My father's blasted brilliant plan to see me wed."

Generally, matters of marriage and prospective brides were the manner of talk gentlemen took pains to avoid—unless they had to. And in Westfield's case, with his father nearing the end of his life, it was a topic that could not be avoided. Not by a friend, at least.

The crack of the cue ball resonated in the quiet room done in crimson and mahogany hues. Richard eyed his shot as it settled closest to the baulk. "I do not envy you your responsibility." At one time, he'd fashioned himself as the marrying sort, but had come to appreciate the singular impossibility of finding the one person who owns your heart, and having that lady's sentiments so closely align that it resulted in that forever love.

His friend made a crude gesture that roused a laugh from Richard. Westfield motioned to him. "Your decision."

Richard picked up the red ball and placed it at the top of the table. Wordlessly, he walked a slow path about the table and then, positioning his cue, struck the red ball. The smooth force of the movement propelled it forward and the red ball knocked the other into a pocket. "Have you selected the lady who will be the future Marchioness of Westfield?"

Westfield respotted the red ball at the top of the table in the black spot and positioned his cue. "My father certainly has an idea who the future Duchess of Somerset will be," he muttered. He struck the cue ball and Richard's ball, in a canon shot, which earned him two points.

A pall descended over the room, and Richard collected his drink and took a slow swallow. Having suffered the loss of his own father, and also having a similarly close-knit family as Westfield's, he knew the pain Westfield was surely in. Richard took his shot. "Who is the fortunate young lady, then?" he asked, infusing dry levity into his tone. For when presented with the topics of death and dying and a gentleman's impending marital state, the latter was always safer.

"The Duke of Wilkinson's daughter." He cast a wry glance at Richard. "Though I have no doubt, he'd have me wed *any* respectable young lady at this point."

Again, the spirited creature bolting through the duke's property slipped into his mind.

A knock sounded at the door and they looked as one as it opened, and a liveried servant stepped inside. The bewigged footman sketched a bow and then cleared his throat. He opened his mouth and then closed it, looking over to Richard.

"You can speak freely," Westfield said with a frown.

The servant nodded. "My lord, His Grace has been seized by another fit."

In an uncharacteristic show of agitation, Westfield raked a hand through his hair. "You've summoned—"

"Dr. Hanson. Yes, my lord. His Grace is asking for you."

Westfield gave a jerky nod and then started for the door, but paused and cast a glance back at Richard. "I am sorry—"

"Go," he urged the other man. "This does not matter." The passing of Richard's father had cemented the inanity of the world in which they lived—a world where summer parties were thrown, and guests donned smiles and schemed to wed powerful peers—all while the world was crumbling down upon a family. "See to your father."

With that, Westfield rushed off and the servant pulled the door closed behind him, leaving Richard alone. Collecting his snifter, he strode over to the rich, mahogany sideboard and grabbed a bottle of brandy, then carried the glass and the crystal decanter over to the high crimson-and-gold winged chairs.

Richard settled into a seat. He downed the content of his glass and then pulled the stopper from the bottle. He proceeded to pour himself another snifter. Cradling the glass between his hands, he stared down into the contents.

Perhaps he should return to his family's country party. In accepting Westfield's invite, he'd grasped at the excuse presented which he might give his brothers and not really thought of anything more than avoiding all sights of Eloise with Lucien. His lips pulled in an involuntary grimace. How very pathetic, indeed. For the truth was, he could not avoid the reality of his circumstances and, more, the reality of Eloise, given the sheer nature of his birth connection to the man Eloise had gone and married.

Nor, if he were being truly honest with himself, did he wish to forget her. Eloise had been, at one time, as close as a sister. At first, there had never been a hint of anything romantic between them. His early relationship with the delicate lady had never extended beyond fishing and racing through the Kent countryside. It had been a friendship that was comfortable, calm and familiar.

And when she'd left for London, in search of a husband, his own low sense of self as that second son of a viscount had quelled all truth on his lips. Instead, he'd stood by and watched her marry another, thinking with the love he carried for her that she was deserving of that title and position; all things he could never give her as a title-less horse breeder.

For ultimately, women always craved more. His lips quirked up in a humorless smile. The sprite racing about the duke's properties was proof of that. Most craved wealth and power and prestige. Just as Lady Nameless had proven earlier that evening.

Richard downed the remaining contents of his glass and reached for the bottle resting at his feet.

Later that evening, Gemma slipped out of her guest bedchambers and closed the door quietly behind her. She peeked down the hall. Finding it blessedly empty, she snuck past door after door.

Even in the still of the night, with no hint of guests about, her heart doubled its beat. Following her discovery at the steward's hands that evening, the risks in seeking out Lord Westfield reared, more real than they'd been before. To be found gallivanting about the duke's property and sneaking about his home, unchaperoned, would result in immediate ruin. Fortunately, Gemma had long escaped Society's notice and was afforded certain freedoms. This, however, would result in the height of scandal from which no lady could recover. If she was found pursuing the marquess…A little shiver shook her frame, and she thrust aside the dire musings. Why, if that were to happen, she might as well don red and declare herself a fallen woman.

And what if you were discovered kissing the nameless steward, all the while shamelessly hungry to know more of that man's embrace?

She forced her ragged breath into a semblance of calm and thrust that coarse stranger from her thoughts and, instead, focused on the most imminent threat. Gemma turned the corner and slammed into a solid wall. Her scream died on her lips. "Emery," she blurted.

Her brother stood with arms folded at his chest eying her with the proper degree of suspicion. "Gemma," he drawled. "What are you doing wandering about at this hour?"

Oh, blast and double blast on Sunday. How to explain her furtive sneaking to a person who'd long known to be wary of that very sneaking? Emery winged an eyebrow upwards. Why could she not have been one of those ladies with clever responses? Instead, she stood, unblinking like a dratted owl perfectly caught by her brother. "Is it late?"

"It is," he repeated, his ever-narrowing eyes conveyed his wariness. "There you are."

Brother and sister swung their gazes as one to Beatrice who stood with her hands propped on her hips and a smile wreathing her guileless face. Salvation came in the most unexpected, but most welcome, form as Beatrice strode forward. The mischievous twinkle sparkling in her cornflower blue eyes belied that perception of innocence.

Some of the tension drained from Gemma.

The consummate gentleman, Emery dropped a bow. "Lady Beatrice."

As though they met in a formal parlor and not in the empty corridors of the duke's largely slumbering household, Beatrice curtsied. "Lord Smithfield, may I steal Gemma away?"

He studied Beatrice through suspicious eyes a moment and with a slow nod, took a step back. "Of course. Please, do not let me interfere with your enjoyments."

Fighting a wave of guilt, Gemma leaned up on tiptoe and pecked her brother on the cheek. "Goodnight, Emery." Then, sliding her arm through Beatrice's, she allowed her friend to lead her onward.

"Gemma?" Her brother called out, bringing the ladies back around. Gemma stared questioningly at him. "Behave."

A guilty heat slapped her cheeks and she mustered a smile. "Don't I always?"

"No," he said automatically, swiftly killing her false grin. "You do not." He touched the brim of an imagined hat. "Lady Beatrice."

The ladies waited a moment and then resumed their path in the opposite direction.

"That was close," Beatrice muttered under her breath, stealing a look over her shoulder. "You must take greater care."

Again, the duke's steward slipped into Gemma's thoughts and her lips tingled with the remembered feel of his mouth on hers. At the peculiar look Beatrice shot her, Gemma forced a response. "I know."

Giving a pleased nod, Beatrice marched them with military-like precision and purpose through her father's sprawling home. They descended the stairs and reached the main landing. Then, all hint of flawless, too-proper miss thrown aside, Beatrice grabbed Gemma by the hand and tugged her along. "You do not have much time," she whispered. "Robert is alone in the billiards room."

Gemma furrowed her brow. Generally, gentlemen retired for drinks with the other men, desiring an escape from polite company. Or, that had been her observation as a younger sister, anyway. It was as though there was some unspoken, unwritten masculine pact among those titled lords to avoid marriage-minded ladies. "Are you certain he's alone?"

"Quite." Glossing over the skepticism in Gemma's question, Beatrice continued. "He takes drinks there by himself. More so since P-Papa..." She coughed into her palm.

Pain tugged at Gemma's heart and she captured her friend's fingers, giving them a slight squeeze. The words "I am sorry" were so absolutely futile and useless when presented with the unspoken sadness blanketing this house.

"Come, none of that," Beatrice said, and winked. "I'd focus on happy things like rainbows and rides through the countryside at midnight and your pursuit of Robert."

A strangled laugh lodged in Gemma's throat. What sorry days, indeed, when a lady was the one to bring a gentleman up to scratch.

She wrinkled her nose. Though, in truth, there was something empowering in seizing control of one's destiny.

Gripping her by the forearms, Beatrice steered Gemma forward. She gave her a slight nudge between the shoulder blades. "Off you go. Third door down the corridor, on the right. Make him see reason."

Gemma frowned. Make him see reason? Wasn't love about illogical thought and maddening passion? The manner of dizzying desire that had gripped her in a stranger's arms. She turned to ask her friend as much, but like a slip of fog rolled back by the morning light, Beatrice disappeared. With a sigh, Gemma forced her legs to move.

If Mother knew Gemma even now crept down the silent, candlelit corridors, seeking out the company of a gentleman…Alone. Unchaperoned. Which, in thinking, really was quite redundant, the whole alone and unchaperoned business…Gemma gave her head a clearing shake. Even nervous in her silent musings.

She paused at the end of the hall. Third door down the corridor, on the right. Third door, on the right. Gemma stole one more glance backward. After all, a person could never be too certain there weren't servants about. Or in the case of the early evening…stewards about. Stewards with firm lips and thick, chestnut hair and wicked, if mocking, grins. Her skin heated as she thrust thoughts of the duke's steward aside and fixated on the task at hand. More importantly, avoiding discovery so she might profess her love, at last.

Holding her breath, Gemma continued on to the billiards room. She would have explaining to do if it were say, Mama and not Emery, who'd found she'd snuck off in the dead of night. "And what would she say if she knew it was all an attempt to see a gentleman—alone?" she mumbled to herself. The dashing, charming brother of her dearest friend but still, a clandestine meeting was a clandestine meeting, and one that were she to be discovered would no doubt find Gemma packed off to an abbey.

But some men were worth braving scandal over and Lord Westfield was one of them.

Yes, he was whispered about as something of a rogue, but surely even a charmer such as he would not go about kissing young women he did not know and grab them closer than ever could be appropriate. Her lips burned from the memory of earlier that evening and she paused in the corridor, touching her fingertips to her lips. Then, gaining control of her thoughts, she refocused on Lord Westfield. She didn't give a fig if he was a duke or destitute. She'd loved him since he'd rescued her from a dance-less debut at Almack's. She'd loved him for being a devoted brother who cared about the happiness of his family, when most lords only cared about wagering and carousing. And she loved him for every kindness he'd shown her through every painful London Season.

Gemma wiped her damp palms along the sides of her wrinkled skirt and continued walking. Except, with each step, her courage deserted her. She touched the handle of the door…and then froze.

What are you doing, Gemma Reed? Young ladies did not steal upon a gentleman who sought privacy, declare their love, and make an absolute cake of themselves all in the hopes that he would return those very sentiments.

It was that small lingering hope that he would, in fact, profess his love that compelled her to press the handle, entering the quiet room. She closed the door behind her so softly the faint click barely registered with her own ears.

It took her eyes a moment to adjust to the darkened billiards room. But for a handful of candles, the thick black of night shrouded the room in an eerie quiet. She searched the grand space adorned in crimson curtains and heavy, red mahogany furniture. She stilled as her gaze found the tall figure seated on the leather winged back chair. As if sensing her presence, Lord Westfield stiffened in profile and then made to rise.

"D-do not!" she called out, and he froze. "Stand, that is." Her voice echoed around the room. Digging deep for the courage to share the words she'd kept silent for too long, she drew in a slow, steadying breath. "It would be easier if you were to sit there for me to say this. To say what it is that I need to say. What I've been longing to say." She flinched at her jumbled ramblings. "You have captivated me since the moment I first met you." Her impassioned declaration echoed off the walls. "From the moment I first saw you smile, I've longed to tell you how good and kind and loyal you are." *He is not a blasted hound, Gemma!*

She took a step forward, appreciating his silence that allowed her the courage to continue. "I would have you know the feelings I've carried." She held her palm up, forgetting a moment that he could not see her. "But I love you. I've loved you for so very long and given the party hosted by your father, I thought you should know how ardently I admire you, as I carry the hope that you might feel the same way, too. You are my heart's greatest yearning."

Gemma cringed at the silence, which met her impassioned profession. Her heart beat loud in her ears. As she waited, breath suspended in her lungs for Lord Westfield to say something. Alas…Gemma shifted on her feet. She'd really settle for anything.

When it became apparent he had little or no intention of saying anything more on it, she cleared her throat. "Will you not say anything to me?" Where did she, so often without words, find the courage to toss that question out to him?

He slowly stood, unfurling to his full height. She swallowed hard and allowed herself one infinitesimal moment to believe the dimly lit room merely played cruel tricks upon her eyes. Except, she blinked.

And then blinked again.

For the man before her, the dark-haired, broad figure was so very different than the blond-haired, charming gentleman she'd sought.

And…

Oh God…

She curled her feet into the soles of her slippers as mortified heat set her body ablaze over the horrifying mistake she'd made. Shame spiraled through her being as a slow smile formed on the steward's hard lips; lips that had covered hers, giving her, her first kiss, earlier that evening.

He sketched a bow. "What is there to say? Other than I'm flattered. Now, may I ask the name of the woman so hopelessly in love with my smile?"

Oh, my God. "No, you may n-not," she squeaked. Gemma winced at that high-pitched, broken utterance. "And I was not commenting on your smile. I don't even know your smile."

The steward leaned against the chair, cradling a drink in his hand. "Well, that is not altogether true."

She groaned. For it wasn't. She did know his smile, just…"Not well," she said tightly. "I've seen but one of your grins."

The steward smiled all the more. Now *two* grins. And even if it was a slightly wicked, slightly teasing, expression, she'd certainly not admire it. Not from a man whose name she did not know, and only just met. Her mind slowed, stalled, and then resumed a rapid spinning pace. Oh, God. "You are not the duke's steward."

Hers was a statement borne of horrified fact.

"I am not," he confirmed, anyway, with yet another of those seductive, teasing grins.

Which could only mean…. "You are a guest?" Please let him be an insolent servant nipping brandy from his employer. Please let him be anyone other than a guest who'd witnessed her two humiliations and who'd kissed her senseless.

"I am, indeed."

Her mind scrambled to put together who this stranger was. Who, when with her three-year friendship with Beatrice, she'd met this man not once. She'd not seen him at a single event. She peered into the dark, up at him, trying to place him.

"I am a friend of—"

Do not say it. Do not say…

"Lord Westfield's." He spread his arms wide. "Mr. Richard Jonas."

Oh, God. He'd said it. Gemma closed her eyes and shook her head despairingly. Of all the rotted luck. Of all the ill-timing and tricks of fate. Then memory of their scandalous first meeting sank through the quagmire of her thoughts. She flared her eyes wide in horror. "You ki—"

"I returned your kiss," he supplied for her. "Yes." He took a step closer. "And it was an enjoyable one, wouldn't you say, sweet?"

His words rang a gasp from her and she ignored that shockingly improper question. Gemma moved in a whir of skirts, placing the billiards table between them. "Returned *my* kiss?" she choked out. He painted her as a wanton and, with his flippant words, made her first kiss

32

something shameful. Granted it *was* scandalous to go about embracing strangers but still, it had been a thing of wonder. Annoyance blended with mortified anger in a violent dance—with him *and* herself. "First," she stuck a finger out. "It takes two to waltz." His lips twitched, only fueling her outrage. "And second," she dropped her voice to a hushed whisper, "*you,* sir, kissed *me.*"

He made a tsking sound and she gritted her teeth. "Ah, disappointed that I was not another?"

She bit the inside of her cheek, willing him to silence.

The gentleman continued coming toward her. "You were searching out a particular gentleman who was..." He winged an eyebrow up and stopped beside her. "Good, kind, and loyal." Another mocking grin pulled at his lips. "You would do very well with a terrier."

Despising that his own mocking thoughts aligned so very shamefully alongside her earlier ones, Gemma's skin burned hot. She dropped her voice to a furious whisper. "You should have alerted me to your presence."

"I did. I made to rise and you urged me to sit."

"Because I believed you were another," she said, exasperation creeping into her tone.

He set the snifter in his hand on the edge of the billiards table, bringing her attention briefly to that very nearly empty glass, and then she jerked her attention back to his. "Regardless, considering I know not only the taste of your lips." He continued over her outraged gasp. "A taste of mint and honey—"

"Mr. Jonas!" She'd never believed even one's ears could go hot with embarrassment.

"I also know your heart's greatest yearning." His lips twitched with amusement and filled with the need to plant the lout a deserved facer, her fingers curled into reflexive balls. "Then at the very least I can know your—"

"My name is Miss Gemma Reed," she gritted out, settling her hands on her hips. After all, there was something wholly wrong in receiving one's first kiss from a complete stranger, and then confessing the most intimate pieces that dwelled inside her heart. "And I am a friend of Lady Beatrice Dennington."

"Then we are a perfect pair, friends both to the Denningtons."

Gemma threw her hands up. "We are nothing. You are an aggravating, infuriating, exasperating—"

"The latter two mean the same."

"Lout. And I'll not stand here and be mocked by a man who should conceal his identity and—"

He dipped his head and swallowed the remaining words with his mouth.

Gemma stilled under this gentle assault, so very different from the explosive meeting of mouths earlier that evening. She fluttered her lids and stretched her hands up. To push him away. Solely to push him away. And yet...

A warm fluttering danced in her belly and a slow heat built inside, growing and spreading until every corner of her being trilled awake at his tender ministrations. Of their own volition, her fingers found purchase in the fabric of his black coat, and she tugged at it, leaning into his kiss.

His kiss.

She froze.

Nay, their kiss.

Her second kiss. Neither of which belonged to Lord Westfield and both belonged to this Mr. Richard Jonas; dryly mocking, and constantly teasing.

Gemma sprung away from him and knocked painfully against the billiard table. The hard mahogany bit into her hip and she welcomed the dull, throbbing ache that served as a distraction from the guilt of her betrayal. She stuck up a quavering finger. "Do not," she rasped, her chest moving hard and fast in time to the frantic beat of her heart.

Except he was stock still, eying her through impossibly long, chestnut lashes, she'd have traded both of her smallest fingers for.

"That should not have happened."

"Because of your heart's greatest yearning?" He lowered his head slightly shrinking the space between them. "Tell me, though, Gemma—"

"I did not give you leave to use my Christian name."

Richard stroked the pad of his thumb over her lower lip and her mouth trembled at the faint caress. "I believe our kisses merit such familiarity." His gruff baritone washed over her, dulling her senses, thickening her blood.

Oh, God, he is going to kiss me—again. This man, more stranger than anything, whose name she'd only just gleaned, and yet who knew so very much about her. "Is your heart's yearning a product of the desire for a future title of duchess or the marquess' wealth?" She'd have to be deaf as a post to fail to hear the thread of mockery underscoring that question.

The momentary fog of desire he'd cloaked her in lifted. A growl of frustration worked up her throat. "You sir, are no gentleman," she seethed and jabbed her finger into the hard wall of his chest. He didn't so much as flinch. Not even a hint that he so much as noted her poke. She shoved her finger into his chest once more for good measure. "I'll have you know that my love for Lord Westfield has nothing to do with the gentleman's wealth or title." Gemma ticked her chin up a notch. "Nor do I expect one such as you to know a jot about the emotion of love. Now, if you'll excuse me." With head held high, Gemma swept past him, pulled the door open, and slipped into the hall.

Except, as she made her hasty flight down the blessedly empty corridors, she could not quell the panicky dread that this was not the last dealing she'd have with Mr. Richard Jonas and his wickedly sensual smile.

FOUR

R ichard hadn't the slightest interest in attending a single morning meal with the Duke of Somerset's carefully selected guests.

That was, until this particular morning. Now, as he strolled down
the elegant carpet-lined corridors, an inexplicable anticipation filled
him. After Eloise had wed his brother, he'd been filled with a jaded restlessness and ennui. In two brief meetings, however, he'd felt a remarkable vigor which, if he were being honest with himself, had everything
to do with the spirited minx who'd boldly returned his kisses.

Richard entered the breakfast room and did a quick search. He
took in the handful of guests seated and involuntarily flinched. Down
the length of one entire end of the table, perched at the edge of their
chairs were a row of young ladies and their mamas. There was only one
particular young lady he particularly cared to see.

Disappointment filled him at finding Gemma Reed absent, which
was, of course, madness. She, in her grasping, was no different than the
white-ruffled ladies eying him disinterestedly. Those same ladies also
sat staring at the doorway for sight of a certain marquess, no doubt,
like rapacious predators.

Richard strode over to the sideboard and accepted the plate
handed him by a footman. With a murmured thanks, Richard proceeded to pile sausage, eggs, and kippers onto his plate. The floorboards groaned and he paused mid-movement. Awareness tripped
along his spine and he shot a look over his shoulder at the lady who now
stood in the doorway. In a manner similar to his own from moments
ago, she cast her gaze over the collection of guests assembled, when

their stares collided. Her cheeks turned a crimson red to rival the most succulent summer berry. She eyed the path behind her. Did she search for Westfield? Or escape?

He'd wager the latter. Yet, when most other ladies would flee, she jutted her chin up and made her way to the sideboard. Richard resumed piling his plate with food. "It appeared you were looking for someone, Miss Reed," he said in hushed tones for her ears alone.

"I was," she said from the corner of her mouth, leaving that thought deliberately unfinished.

She added a piece of bread to her plate and then froze. "You cannot possibly be eating that, Mr. Jonas?"

He followed her horror struck gaze to the smoked kipper with a poached egg atop. Bristling, he added another kipper for good measure. "Have you ever had kippers, Miss Reed?"

She snorted. "Undoubtedly not."

"And yet, given how little you truly know about the kipper, you've formed such an ardent feeling for it."

Her eyes narrowed into thin slits of understanding. The spirit lighting their depths transformed her from an ordinary miss with brown hair and brown eyes into a feisty minx needing a third kiss, momentarily robbing him of thought. "I know quite a bit about the kipper," she said tightly, angling so she directly faced him. "It is a whole herring and it is small, oily, found in fresh waters, and..." She wrinkled her nose. "They smell. Quite badly."

Richard met her stare full on. "Those are very detailed pieces of information you have..." He gave her a meaningful look. "On the kippers. It *is*, however, information that can be gleaned by anyone."

They stood, locked in a silent battle with their chests rising and falling—when the absolute silence registered.

A flush heated his neck and raced up to his ears as from the corner of his eye, he noted the gaping members of the peerage taking in his exchange with Gemma. The color of her skin turned red and if he weren't close to yanking his cravat at the attention on him, he'd have looked with an even greater appreciation upon the splash of color on the skin exposed above her modest décolletage. Instead, his gaze snagged on the familiar figure in the doorway. And just like that, all the attention trained on a mere Mr. Richard Jonas and Miss Gemma Reed was forgotten at the sudden appearance of Westfield. A buzz went up about the room and Richard inclined his head. "Miss Reed, you might wish to try the kipper before they are claimed by all the other guests."

Another spirited glimmer lit the lady's eyes but then with the regal bearing of a queen, Gemma marched over to the table. A young footman pulled out a chair and she slid into the folds with a quiet thank you. Richard carried his dish beside her. She placed the crisp white napkin on her lap and then stilled "What are you doing?"

"Sitting," he returned, and even as she opened her mouth, he claimed the mahogany chair.

As Westfield made his way to the sideboard, each young lady present and her mama, followed him with their eyes. Interestingly, all except the very one who'd risk her good name and ruin, who now occupied the chair next to his. The lady devoted her attention to her plate, moving the silver fork around the contents upon the white, gold-trimmed porcelain.

He studied her with renewed interest; the silenced magpie now sat huddled within herself, shoulders bent as though she sought to disappear within herself.

Westfield looked over the table a moment and then strode over. The young ladies present held their breaths, and then let out a collective sigh of disappointment as he came to a stop not at the head—but beside that brown-haired, silenced magpie. "May I claim this seat?" Westfield favored the top of Gemma's head with a charming grin that was wasted on the young woman who still examined the toast on her plate as though she'd uncovered a new genus of flower.

Then her shoulders went straight and she looked about. Richard repressed a frown as the lady locked her gaze with Westfield's. He searched for the excited ramblings or the clever words and, yet, the long case clock in the corner of the room ticked by the incredibly long stretch of awkward silence.

Richard took mercy. Under the table, he nudged his knee against Gemma's and she jumped. He gave her a meaningful look and she blinked several times before saying, "Of course. That would be most permissible, my lord." The lady swiftly returned her attention to that damnable piece of toast that she now set to buttering.

Most permissible? Richard furrowed his brow and stared openly at his friend who claimed the chair on Gemma's opposite side. Who was this reserved, guarded creature? Why, she didn't display a shadow of the spirited miss who'd kissed him with abandon and challenged him at the sideboard before a room full of guests.

Westfield leaned over and murmured something close to Gemma's ear and a rush of the becoming color flooded her cheeks. The lady nodded, but her response was lost to Richard.

His frown deepened. Why, by the devil, Westfield was...*flirting* with the young lady. A little pebble of what felt like annoyance pitted in his belly. It was preposterous, unthinkable, it was...He gave his head a hard shake. Why in blazes should he care who the other man settled his attentions on? And he most assuredly should not care.

With zeal, Richard carved away at his kipper. Small and oily, indeed. He popped a piece into his mouth and the lady stole a sideways peek. He chewed and stared boldly back at her, daring her with his gaze to say something.

Gemma captured her lower lip between her teeth. She wished to say something about his choice of meal and there was something very oddly...intimate about knowing that about this lady.

Instead, she shifted her focus back to her plate and remained silent, and as much as Gemma Reed had grated on his last nerve, he also despised seeing her subdued as she was now. With an unexplainable need to draw her from the close-mouthed shell she'd crawled within, he leaned close to say something in her ear when loud voices sounded in the hallway, followed by exuberant tittering. At his side, Gemma jerked erect.

He glanced up as a pair of perfectly golden, undoubtedly flawless, young ladies filed into the room like noisy geese and rushed over to the open seat beside Westfield, quarreling publically over that empty chair.

Gemma slunk low within the folds of her seat and Richard's intrigue with the lady redoubled. Who was Miss Gemma Reed, exactly? Bold, spirited minx? Or painfully shy, quiet miss?

And why did he have this sudden need to know?

Gemma was a bumbling, soundless fool, is what she was.

With Lady Thelma and Lady Constance, twin sisters and soon to be Diamonds of the First Water having settled on just which of them would claim the chair beside Lord Westfield, they proceeded to speak over one another in their bid to capture the young marquess' attention. Where other ladies had the ability to fill voids of silence with clever banter and repartee, Gemma's tongue became tied worse than a sailor's knot.

The singular interest in the marquess and ability to capture his attention should have grated. She stole a sideways glance up at the other gentleman who occupied the chair next to hers. Yet, there was something...oddly reassuring in this near stranger's company. Where she'd never been possessed of words around...well, really any gentleman, with this man she was comfortable in ways she'd never believed possible. He was aggravating and insufferable, and stirred her spirit with his high-handedness.

Why are you thinking of the Marquess of Westfield's friend? Why, when you are seated beside Lord Westfield himself? Giving her head a shake, and then a second one for good measure, she smoothed her hands over the arms of her chair. *I am capable of discourse.* Hadn't she just blistered Richard Jonas' ears at the buffet, handling her rebuttal to his cheeky charges with great aplomb?

"Do you ride, Lord Westfield?" As soon as the inquiry escaped her lips, she cringed; one of those inward and outward types for all to see. Of course he rode. It was rumored that he had one of the most distinguished stables in the kingdom.

The marquess looked to her with a gentle smile and she hated that smile. She would have preferred it to be slightly teasing or even greatly teasing, the way it would have been on a certain Richard Jonas. "I do. I actually have plans to ride following the morning meal."

"I ride," she blurted. Blast, now he'd think she was angling to accompany him. Mortification curled her toes. "Not that I wish to ride with you."

A sound that might have been a strangled laugh escaped Richard at Gemma's opposite side. Oh, the lout. Her neck heated. "Forgive me," she said quickly. "I would certainly enjoy riding with you. I have always loved horses." Horses and dogs were a good deal easier to speak to than the human sort. She cast a desperate look about for Beatrice. Alas, she'd long proven to keep late morning hours, and to avoid a gathering of dowry-seeking lords, at all costs.

Westfield settled back in his seat and layered his arms upon his chair. "You are knowledgeable of horses, then?" He directed that question to the top of her head and she followed his gaze to a stone-faced Richard.

"Oh, yes," she said excitedly, returning her focus to the marquess. This was, after all, a conversation she was familiar with. From across the table, where her mother now sat, she gave her head a curt shake. Ignoring the pleading in her eyes, Gemma leaned forward in her chair. "Really quite fascinating creatures." She gestured wildly with her hands as she spoke. "I once read you can tell a horse's age by his teeth."

"Is that so?" The marquess lifted a golden brow. "What other fascinating pieces do you know?"

"Well, not his precise age," she clarified. "But rather a general estimate of it. They can live to over thirty and did you know..." She dropped her elbows on the table. "It takes over eleven months for a foal to develop inside a mare. And sometimes the foal will arrive early, but it can also arrive as long as four weeks longer. Can you imagine that? Twelve months of—"

"Gemma," her mother's sharp tone cut across Gemma's telling.

And it was then that Gemma registered the gazes of each guest present turned on her as though she were an oddity on display and, in this instance, she was…a display of her own making, borne of topics that were never appropriate for the breakfast table, or any table, for that matter.

Gemma retrained her stare on the eggs on her plate and as the guests returned to topics that moved beyond horse gestation, she shoved her fork around the plate and contemplated it. She could not swallow a single bite. Her stomach churned in a painful knot as she prayed for this moment to end.

Richard leaned close in his chair and it groaned in slight protest. Gemma braced for his coolly mocking words. "Do you know what I also find interesting about horses, Gemma?"

She hesitated and then, not allowing him the triumph of his amusement with her displeasure, bit out, "What is that, Mr. Jonas?"

"Horses cannot vomit or breathe through their mouths."

Gemma stared unblinking at her plate. Surely he hadn't just…? Then she snapped her shoulders back and glared at him. The boiling anger within was far safer than the humiliated embarrassment of her impolite discourse this morning. "Tell me, Mr. Jonas, do you delight in tormenting all young ladies? Or is that pleasure reserved for me?"

A frown marred his lips. "I didn't—"

She angled her body in a way that they were directly facing one another. "But I find nothing kind in your taking pleasure in another person's discomfort."

He opened his mouth. But wanting to hear a single other word from his lips about as much as she wanted to listen to the clever prattling of Lady Thelma who occupied the seat beside the marquess, Gemma shoved back her chair. "I bid you good morning, sir, and hope you find something else to occupy your time other than taunting and tormenting young, more than slightly awkward ladies."

Giving a toss of her hopelessly uncurled hair, she dislodged a strand and it fell flatly over her eye. Then, with her head held high, Gemma marched from the breakfast room. Her feet twitched with the urge to take flight, but where could young ladies steal off to escape any further notice or embarrassments?

FIVE

The lady had thought he was making light of her.

Given their previous two exchanges, Richard could certainly understand just why Gemma Reed would come to that very opinion. And yet, as he guided his mount over the duke's rolling property, that very low opinion she carried grated. For that exchange had singularly revealed more of anything real about the lady than any other words she'd uttered.

Until the morning meal, she'd been nothing more than any other lady present, hunting a future-duke and professing love based on flimsy words better reserved for a hound. Then she'd gone on one of her endearing rambles and she'd swiftly become a lady with interests... and what was more, she'd become a lady with an interest in horseflesh.

For all the shock and disgust etched in the faces of the assembled guests, Richard had been...his eye twitched. By God, he'd been captivated by the little minx in that instant. He clenched and unclenched his jaw. Only, the lady had seen him as judgmental as every other member of the peerage present.

And why shouldn't she? You've done nothing but bait and tease her since the moment she stepped into your riding path a day prior.

Guilt needled at him and he urged Warrior onward. He scanned his gaze over the lush, green, rolling countryside. Where would a lady escape? No doubt the last person she cared to see in this moment was him. A memory of her as she'd been, with humiliated hurt blazing in her eyes, caused a knot in his belly. He far preferred the lady snapping and hissing like a cornered cat than the dejected, slumped figure who'd hastily fled the breakfast room.

Richard slowed his mount to a stop and Warrior danced in a small circle. He patted the horse's damp coat and glanced in the direction of the lake. With a click of his tongue, he wheeled Warrior around and cantered on to the thick copse at the edge of the duke's property. He guided Warrior to a stop and then, with reins in hand, walked the massive creature over to nearby brush and looped his reins about a thin oak. Patting him once on the withers, he strode over to the copse, and then hesitated.

What was the likelihood the lady was even here? He turned to go when a faint sniffling penetrated the morning quiet. Perhaps it was just the rustling leaves overhead. Or perhaps it was…

Sniff Sniff

That muffled sound of misery cleaved through him. Unhesitant, Richard entered the copse, moving deeper into the densely wooded area and then stopped. Gemma sat atop a boulder with her knees drawn close to her chest. The sight of her tucked against herself, with her shoulders bent, wrenched at something in him. He took a step forward and a branch snapped loudly in the quiet.

Gemma froze and then whipped her head around. "You."

In the absolute absence of anger or outrage in that tone, he took another step forward. "Me."

She dropped her legs over the edge of her sitting place and hopped to her feet. "I did not come here to be mocked by you. I have suffered through enough of your company these two days, Mr. Jonas." A fiery glimmer lit her brown eyes and they sparkled with such spirit, words momentarily left him. She narrowed her gaze. "Why are you staring at me like that?"

And because he really didn't care to examine why he'd been staring at her and just what she made of that look, Richard touched a hand to his chest. "Richard," he corrected her.

"I beg your pardon?" Four little creases lined her brow.

"My name is Richard." It defied propriety, and the cool dislike that had existed since their first meeting, but he wished to hear his name on her lips. He desperately wished to hear her wrap those two syllables in her lilting tone. *I'm going utterly mad. There is no else accounting for it.* "I did not come here to mock you." Once again, guilt needled at him. For the lady was certainly entitled to her suspicious opinion where he was concerned.

"Do you mean you have not come here to mock me more than you have already done these past two days?" She shot an eyebrow up and guilty heat burned his neck. "No," she scoffed. "I hardly need you to point out everything inappropriate in speaking on a horse's gestation, at the breakfast table, no less," she muttered that last part under her breath.

No there wasn't anything appropriate in such discourse. It was, however, the singularly most interesting thing any woman of his acquaintance had uttered...including Eloise. For her love of riding, she'd feared horses, and certainly hadn't known a jot about their teeth or gestational period. He'd *seen* only Eloise for so long, he'd failed to appreciate that there were any women with an interest in the equine. And there was something...really rather captivating about a woman with that shared interest. A smile pulled at his lips. Lest she see it and again believe he made light of her, Richard promptly schooled his features. "I understand I've given you little reason to trust me."

"No you haven't," she shot back, and a strand of hair fell over her brow. An urge grew to take that lock between his fingers and test whether the tresses that shimmered in the sunlight streaming through the dancing leaves overhead were as satiny soft as it appeared. She shoved it behind her ear, stealing that opportunity from him. Gemma advanced. "First, you kissed me."

Which he'd greatly enjoyed. He retreated a step.

"Then," she stretched out that single syllable. "Despite knowing I mistook you for another gentleman..." Which he did not like at all, for reasons that he also did not know or care to examine. Color flooded her cheeks. "You allowed me to bare my heart's y—" This would assuredly be an inappropriate place to smile. He fixed on thoughts of their kisses and the satiny smoothness of her skin. Desirous musings that would kill all amusement. He swallowed a groan. Mayhap that was not the safest direction, after all. "Furthermore, Mr. Jonas," she contin-ued as she took another step. "You allowed me to confess secrets I've shared with only my dearest friend."

He scowled. In knowing she'd spoken of Westfield with another, made her declaration to the gentleman…something more. Something unpleasant, indefinable, roiled in his belly. "You urged me to remain seated."

Throwing her hands up, she emitted an exasperated sigh. "Because I believed you were Lord Westfield." Which made her interest in Westfield even *more* real, and he didn't quite know what to make of the odd tightening in his chest at that truth. She jabbed a long, gloveless finger in his chest, drawing his attention to the digit. "Then you spoke of horse vomit." This lively figure before him was so vastly different than the shy, hesitant lady in the breakfast room. He far preferred her spitting and sparkling to the subdued miss she'd been earlier. It was a crime that a woman with her spirit should ever be so silenced.

"I am a horse breeder."

Gemma opened her mouth to speak and then closed it. "What?" She tipped her head at an endearing angle.

Richard encircled her slender wrist within his fingers and removed it from his person. "I am a horse breeder," he said again. "I suspected a lady knowledgeable about horse teeth and the gestational period of the creatures would appreciate that piece of information." For as direct and unflinching as she'd been, speaking amidst the assembled guests, there had been nothing that marked her as squeamish. Rather, she'd spoken with a zeal that had…intrigued him.

Some of the fight seeped from her tautly held frame. "A horse breeder?"

He didn't believe it bore repeating a third time and, yet, for the lady's benefit he nodded anyway.

She leaned up on tiptoe and peered at him. He shifted under her focus. Did she believe his profession should be stamped on his skin? Then, she smiled. A genuine grin devoid of mockery and, instead, full of wonder. "A horse breeder."

That truth had been met with either disdain or disinterest from ladies of the peerage through the years. He didn't know what to make of this slow, approving smile that, by the sheer honesty of it, contradicted all his earliest misgivings and suspicions of Miss Gemma Reed.

He cleared his throat, suddenly uncomfortable with seeing her in any way other than the title-hunting schemer who sought to maneuver a meeting with Westfield. For if he'd been wrong about the lady in this regard, then she became a person he…well, a person he could very well like. Richard smoothed his palms down the front lapels of his jacket. "If you'll excuse me," he said stiffly. "I will leave you now." He made a bow. "It was not my intention to force you to suffer through my presence any more than you already have." He turned on his heel and started from the copse.

"Wait." her softly spoken request brought him to a stop.

From their first meeting, with all the confounded, inexplicable fluttering caused by his kiss aside, Mr. Richard Jonas had been…well, a proverbial thorn in her side. A gentleman who, with his mocking grin and baiting, she really hadn't much liked. As such, she'd quickly judged his whisperings in her ear a short while ago at the breakfast table as an effort to mock her. But he hadn't. Instead, he'd been…why goodness, he'd been trying to rescue her from abject humiliation.

He wheeled about to face her. This man she hadn't much liked and she now stared at him through newly opened eyes. Towering over her and with his sharply chiseled features, he was, despite her first and hastily formed opinion—really quite handsome. Which mattered not as much as the discovery of this new and unexpected kindness in the gentleman. Richard arched a chestnut eyebrow up.

A guilty flush suffused her cheeks and she scuffed the earth with the tip of her boot. "I was of an erroneous opinion." How coolly polite that sounded. She cleared her throat. "I believed you were making light of me and reacted defensively, and for that, I apologize." How was it that she, who was singularly unable to string together two sentences amidst Polite Society, should speak so unabashedly before this man?

He took a step in her direction. There should have been an unease in being alone in his presence. Though a friend of Lord Westfield, she knew Richard Jonas not at all beyond a handful of meetings. Still, for that, there was an ease in being around him that she'd never experienced with any other gentleman. "And I judged you also in unfairness."

His words yanked her from her inexplicable musings. "Mr. J— Richard," she amended at the piercing gaze he trained on her.

"Given the purpose of the duke's summer party and your own attempts to secure a private meeting with Westfield, I gathered your intentions were driven by nothing more than an interest in that respective title." The wind whipped her hair and that recalcitrant strand danced before her eyes. He took in that limp lock a moment. "It has become apparent that I was incorrect in my suppositions and for that, I apologize," he murmured. He closed the distance between them and the intense glint in his gray eyes momentarily stole her breath.

"I—"

He shot a hand out and with that slight movement went coherent thought. Richard collected that strand of hair and rubbed it between his thumb and forefinger, and there was such a beautifully sweet intimacy in that almost caress. For she, who'd long bemoaned the dullness of the hopelessly flat, refusing to curl, strands, felt almost beautiful for them in that moment. Then, as though she'd merely imagined the appreciation there, he tucked the strand behind her ear and let his arm fall to his side.

Her skin heated with the embarrassment of making more of that action than there was. Still, they were not the snapping, snarling strangers they'd been since their first meeting. For all the errors on both of their parts, there had been much she'd shared with Richard Jonas and for that, she would have a truce with him. She held her fingers out. "My name is Gemma Reed. I prefer horses and dogs to people." The ghost of a smile played on his firm lips. "I am Lord Smithfield's sister and I have had three, soon to be four, miserable Seasons."

Richard looked at her bemusedly and she stood there so long with her hand outstretched and the moments ticking by that a slow-building embarrassment grew within her. She made to lower her arm when he quickly claimed her palm in his. "My name is Richard Jonas. I am the brother of Viscount Hereford. I breed horses and I'm here at the Duke of Somerset's summer party as a guest of Lord Westfield." Gemma stared at her smaller, delicate fingers dwarfed in his large, callused palm. Olive-hued and slightly coarse from his work, there was a masculine rawness to that hand which caused a thousand butterflies to dance within her belly.

Then his words registered. Lord Westfield. The man she'd loved for years, whom she would confess her feelings to.

Gemma quickly pulled her hand free. She should let him leave and, more, she should return to the estate for the afternoon festivities planned for the day. Instead, reluctant to go back and face the awkward humiliation of mingling in a world in which she'd never felt to belong, she asked, "How long have you known Lord Westfield?" Because surely questions about the man she hoped to marry were permitted and safe reasons to remain shut away in this copse with a man who was decidedly not the marquess.

"We attended Eton as children. He never minded that I was merely the second son of a viscount and I didn't give a jot that he would inherit a dukedom. It was a natural friendship."

Yes, that was the manner of man Lord Westfield was; one who didn't preen and brag for his title before lesser lords. Yet, all she could focus on was Richard as he would have been, a young boy of perhaps seven or eight, shunned by members of the *ton* who, in fact, saw him as lesser. As the unmarried, unsought after daughter of a viscount, she could well identify with what it was to be so casually dismissed by the peerage.

"They are not always the kindest, are they?" she said quietly.

He inclined his head. "I prefer the company of horses and dogs."

They shared a smile and the slight connection forged a gentle bond between them. Which only reminded her that he was here...with her…when the other gentlemen had intended to ride. She cleared her throat. "I expect you wish to rejoin the other gentlemen on the hunt."

He appeared as though he wished to say something, but then sketched another bow. "And I will leave you to your thoughts, madam." Except, he didn't leave. He remained fixed there with a handful of paces between them. She studied him expectantly. Richard beat his palm against his thigh. "There is no need for you to be anything other than yourself…in Westfield's presence," he added as more of an afterthought. "Westfield will appreciate your sincerity and lack of fawning." With that, he turned on his heel once more and stalked from the copse.

Gemma stood staring after Richard long after he'd left, not knowing what to do with this gentleman who saw past the nervous, oft silent, and then stammering girl seen by the rest of the *ton*.

SIX

Seated in the Duke of Somerset's library with the express intention of avoiding the evening's festivities, the more Richard peered into the contents of his snifter, the more he studied the droplets clinging to the side of the glass. And the longer he stared at the contents, the more he appreciated that if one studied the French liquor in just the right way, it bore a remarkable similarity to Gemma Reed's eyes.

With a strangled sound, Richard swilled the remaining spirits.

Footsteps sounded in the hall and he glanced up just as Westfield pushed the door open and stepped inside. He took in the snifter in Richard's hands and closed the door behind him. "I suspected I might find you closeted away with my well-stocked sideboard," he said, not breaking his stride as he made his way over to that very mahogany piece of furniture.

Seated in the folds of the leather winged back chair, Richard shifted in his seat. His friend spoke as though Richard was one of those drink-indulgent carousers.

Westfield touched the edge of the bottle to his glass and the clink of crystal hitting crystal filled the room. "Will you attend the evening recital?"

Once again, Richard stared at those nearly brown droplets clinging to his glass. What manner of singing voice would Miss Gemma Reed possess? He'd wager she sung with a gusto and passion...but then his smile slipped. *I prefer the company of horses and dogs...*

But then, a lady treated so unkindly by Society, a woman who would bury her gaze in her plate and stammer through discourse, was one who'd not sing with such abandon. Not on display, as was expected of ladies of the *ton*. When alone, however, she no doubt sang with great zeal and a carefree, unbridled passion…

Westfield cleared his throat.

She would be the manner of lady who secretly rode astride and galloped through the countryside with the wind whipping at that same belligerent brown tress and—

Westfield again made a clearing sound.

Richard stared unblinkingly at his glass and then raised his gaze to where his friend stood eying him perplexedly. Fighting the urge to tug at his cravat, Richard set his glass aside. "I will join your recital."

His friend snorted. "It is hardly my recital." Then he rolled his glass between his fingers. "Just an event by which the young ladies assembled by my father can be presented to display the worth of their candidacy as future duchess." His lips pulled in a cynical, humorless smile.

Gemma flitted through his thoughts. Richard drummed his fingertips on the arm of his chair. Given the heartbreak Westfield had suffered at another woman's hands, he'd celebrate a pairing that saw the young marquess happy. So what was this selfish yearning to have Westfield choose another rather than the clever Gemma Reed? "Tell me. Is there a certain young lady who might, indeed, fit that role of future duchess?" He infused a deliberate boredom into his tone. After all, it wouldn't do to seem interested in whether a certain lady with brown hair and brown eyes had, indeed, garnered Westfield's notice.

"There is—"

Whatever there was or was not, Richard would never know because the door was thrown open and Lady Beatrice spilled into the room. Both men promptly came to their feet.

"Robert, there you are," she said, slightly breathless, and her heaving chest hinted at the quick pace the lady had no doubt set for herself. "The recital is set to begin and I…" She staggered to a stop and looked between Richard and her brother. "Oh, Mr. Jonas," she said and dropped her gaze demurely.

"Lady Beatrice," he said politely and dropped a bow.

She smiled. "Forgive me, it was not my intention to interrupt your meeting. The recital will begin shortly, and..." She returned her attention to her brother. "I thought you might join me in the recital hall and sit beside Gemma and me."

The marquess downed the contents of his glass. "Of course," he said with the brotherly devotion he'd demonstrated to the young lady through the years.

Richard lowered his eyebrows at the lady's less than subtle attempt at matchmaking. Were her efforts a result of her own attempts or did she work on behalf of Gemma Reed? And why should it matter either way?

Casting a regretful look back, Westfield held out his elbow for his sister. The pair stopped at the door. "Changed your mind about joining the *fun*?" The dry humor in that last word earned him an elbow in the side.

"On the contrary," he replied automatically. "I am quite looking forward to it." It was hard to say who was more shocked by that concession; Richard himself, or Westfield who eyed him, mouth agape.

"Splendid," Lady Beatrice said with a cheerful smile. "Come along, then. I promised Gemma I would not leave her to her own devices."

There was a complete selfishness in accepting an invite and removing himself from all the respective and respectable events planned for the week. That is what he told himself as he fell into step behind Westfield and his sister. How else was there to account for the willingness and, more, desire to attend an infernal recital with marriageable misses in the market for a husband?

"...Do be nice to her," Lady Beatrice was saying to her brother.

With no doubt about the identity of the "her" in question, Richard carefully attended the discourse.

"Have I ever been anything but nice to the lady?" Westfield's dry whisper earned another nudge from his sister.

"Behave. You know the *ton* is cruel to her."

Westfield's hushed response was lost to him and his gut clenched. He'd long despised the world of Polite Society. Theirs was a glittering falseness where titles reigned supreme and worth was decided by one's possession of or linkage to those titles. As a viscount's second son, he'd been spared the disdain Lady Beatrice spoke of but he had, by his birthright as spare to the heir, known that disinterest. In truth, he'd quite welcomed that imposed distance presented by Society. For Gemma, however, she'd been received with cruelty; jeered and mocked, even *with* her rank as viscount's daughter. No doubt, the *ton* preferring ladies who prattled about the weather and Society events failed to see Gemma Reed as an original with a keen wit.

And he found himself despising those pompous lords and ladies for having treated her so through the years, and equally hating himself for having mocked her since their first exchange. He came to a slow stop and stared blankly down the hall. Through his actions, he'd neatly placed himself alongside those who'd been cruel to her. He curled his hands into tight fists. What a horrible, humbling moment.

"Jonas?"

Richard started and looked to where Westfield and Lady Beatrice stood outside of the recital hall. A dull flush climbed his neck and he hastily made his way to the room.

"I thought you'd changed your mind, after all," Westfield said with a grin.

He inclined his head. "I am going to occupy a row at the back of the room."

Before Westfield could reply, Lady Beatrice fixed a firm stare on her brother. "Blast, we are too late. Gemma is already seated. You are decidedly not leaving me to be on display in this room."

He chucked her under the chin. "Never."

As brother and sister made their way into the room, Richard passed his gaze over the neatly arranged chairs. Most of the guests had already assembled and now sat in their perfect rows, with heads craned back. They gawked with a shameful notice at the duke's offspring, the way powerful lords surveyed the horseflesh in Richard's stables. All gazes were trained on the pair, except one particular bent head.

Gemma occupied the last seat in her row, speaking with a blond gentleman, near in age to Richard. Through their discourse, she periodically nodded and said something back that earned a chuckle. The easy familiarity between them spoke of a close, sibling relationship.

Richard walked behind the duke's children, who claimed shell-backed chairs in the first row beside the pale Duke of Somerset. The man's drawn features and the pain in his blue eyes hinted at the effects of his wasting illness. A wave of sadness ran through him. A little over two years ago, his own father had died so, with pain, and desiring to see closure to his time on earth. For his suffering, and the freedom death had brought to that suffering, the loss was still sharp. It reminded one of the brevity of life and the foolishness of wasting one's time with these inane events. He turned to go when Gemma picked her head up. She angled her neck and did a quick search of the room.

He stood transfixed as her deep, brown eyes went to Westfield. The other man said something that brought color to her cheeks and an unpleasant knot tightened in Richard's belly. Something that felt...he blinked...why, remarkably like jealousy. Which was utter madness. The lady didn't much like him. He frowned. That wasn't altogether true. Not any longer. Not following their lakeside meeting in which the lady had dashed his every negative misconception of a woman desiring a title of duchess.

Gemma slid her gaze away from Westfield and, from across the makeshift auditorium, their stares collided. He lifted his head in silent greeting and an unabashed smile turned her lips. It was one of those sincere, joyous expressions not commonly evinced by ladies of the *ton* and it momentarily froze him.

Her brother again said something and, with a slowness hinting at reluctance, she returned her attention to the gentleman at her side. That jerked Richard into motion. He walked to the left of the grand gold parlor and claimed the furthest left seat in the entire room.

Adjusting the tails of his jacket, he slid into the chair preparing to endure the torture of the evening's performances by those ladies in attendance. Except, as Lady Beatrice took her place at the grand piano at the center of the room, Richard's attention remained solely focused on one small, slender form shifting back and forth in her seat.

What was the lady thinking?

In her readings of scientific books deemed inappropriate by Mother, Gemma had come across a fascinating natural phenomenon in the Americas in which the earth shook with such ferocity that for months after, those aftershocks were still felt. Just then, with her mother casting glances her way, Gemma quite knew the only thing saving her from subjecting herself to the self-torture of performing this evening was one of those sizeable events.

Beatrice's soaring lyric soprano filled the room—crisp, clear, beautiful. In short, everything Gemma was not. Oh, she was not so envious that she'd begrudge her friend that talent. Nor did she even wish for a great deal of that aptitude for her own. Why, Gemma would settle for her voice not cracking while she sang. If that was what one truly wished to call it.

As Beatrice brought her song to an impressive finish, the room erupted into more than polite clapping. Gemma ignored the way her mother leaned forward in her chair and gave Gemma a meaningful look. *You are going to perform...* She held her breath but then saints love her friend, Beatrice launched into another song. Through her flawless playing and singing, Gemma shot her gaze about the parlor.

Perhaps she didn't truly need a natural disaster such as the earth quaking. She could very well feign a megrim, or...she chewed her lower lip. Why, she could swoon from her seat. She sighed. Then, she'd never been the elegant, graceful swooning sorts. Where other skilled ladies had long practiced and perfected that not-quite-an-art faint, Gemma had attempted it *once* as a girl. All she'd received was a bloodied nose for her efforts. In this moment, however, the whole swooning business would prove a remarkably handy, certainly beneficial, skill.

Or she could...Or...Blast. She'd not a single worthy scheme to get her out of this inevitable humiliation. Gemma shifted in her seat and discreetly angled her head back, eying the path of escape.

Yes, she was only looking to the doorway. And most assuredly not for...

Richard.

He sat in the last row of the parlor with his gaze trained forward. With his arms folded at his chest, his biceps strained the fabric of his elegant, black evening coat. There, with certain humiliation moments away, she no longer fixed on potential escape but on the sheer broad size of him. With his thick, unfashionably long chestnut hair he had the look of a warrior of old, or Viking or...

Clapping filled the hall and, heart pounding, Gemma yanked her attention forward.

And promptly ignored her pointedly frowning mama. She looked all about; at the sconces lining the walls, up at the mural upon the ceiling done in pastel pinks, purples, and blues, with dancing cherubs and...

"Gemma," her mother snapped, none-too-subtly, and Gemma jerked her head to position with such force she wrenched the muscles in her neck.

"I am certain the audience would greatly prefer another performance from...from Lady Beatrice." Or any other person present.

Alas, Lady Thelma had already hopped to her feet and rushed to the front of the room to claim her spot at the piano. As she proceeded to play, Gemma looked on. The haunting strains of Mozart's *Ave verum corpus* echoed from the walls and danced around her mind. All these ladies assembled, brought together to vie for the marquess. By sheer nature of his future title and power, life with him would bring with it one of constant attention and public scrutiny. The lady he chose as his wife would serve as hostess for dreadful *ton* events. In all her musings of a marriage to Lord Westfield, she'd carefully omitted any such intrusions into the life that included anything but they two.

She looked to Beatrice, now seated beside her father and brother. Was this cloying, suffocating world one she truly wished to belong to? With his devotion to his family and the kindness of his soul, Lord Westfield was a man worthy of enduring that misery.

So why did it feel that thought was half-hearted and belated?

"You know she's going to force you to perform?"

She started at her brother's whisper. Gemma bit down hard on the inside of her cheek. "I could feign a swoon."

Emery winked. "You were always a rotten actress."

Gemma sighed. There was all number of things she'd proven rotten at, to their mother's consternation.

"But do you know what?" Emery said quietly.

She looked questioningly at him.

"You are clever and ride better than most gentlemen I know and are more worthy than any of the ladies here this week."

Emotion clogged her throat. "Thank you," she said softly. He'd always been hopelessly loyal in his regard. When their father had passed almost ten years earlier, Emery had stepped into the role of viscount and been in ways, both brother and de facto father to her thirteen-year-old, gangly, awkward self.

Polite applause went up for Lady Thelma, signaling the end of her set.

"And if I could, you know I would save you this unpleasantness?"

She furrowed her brow.

"Gemma, it is your turn to sing," her mother said loudly and the sharp command echoed in the quiet, bouncing off the walls. Whispers went up about the room.

Oh, God, please let the earth quake, or the floor open or... Her skin burning from the attention trained on her, Gemma swallowed hard. She could not. Her brother gave her a commiserative look and Beatrice matched that show of support from the front row, smiling gently at her.

Bloody hell and damn. Feeling not unlike one being forced to march those final doomed steps to the guillotine, Gemma shoved to her feet and with her shoulders back, walked the short distance to the piano. She stood beside the massive black instrument and stared blankly at the pearl white keys.

Ten years. Ten years she'd been tortured with lessons upon this bloody instrument, and she was as unremarkable and unskilled now as she'd been a girl of twelve first sitting at their modest pianoforte. A nervous giggle bubbled up her throat. It was a shame Society did not judge the merit of a lady on her equine knowledge or her understanding of those earthquakes she still desperately prayed would save her from—

Mother cleared her throat loudly and Gemma jumped. Skin heating, Gemma dropped a curtsy and, averting her gaze from the crowd, she slid onto the bench. The delicate wood groaned in slight protest as she shifted back and forth. Fingers poised over the keyboard, she began to play the lilting tune. Or it would have been properly lilting if a skilled performer such as Beatrice or Lady Thelma now sat. Alas, she stumbled over the keys. Fixing her attention on her task, she shut out the watching eyes of the Duke of Somerset's guests.

Because the longer she shut them out, the more it was as though they were not even present, as though it was simply her galloping over the countryside with her books in her packs, free of judgment, free of Society, free of it all.

> *"Thou bonnie wood of Craigielee,*
> *Thou bonnie wood of Craigielee,*
> *Near thee I've spent life's early day,*
> *And won my Mary's heart in thee…"*

Gemma's voice cracked and a snickering went through the crowd. And she made the mistake of looking out across the hall to the sea of gaping, gawking peers. At the front sat Lord Westfield, a gentle smile of encouragement on his lips. Gemma drew a breath mid-chorus and proceeded through the remainder of the Scottish tune. That is why she'd loved him, because he'd always smiled at her when others had sneered.

> *"Tho' fate should drag me south the line,*
> *Or o'er the wide Atlantic sea,*
> *The happy hours I'll never mind,*
> *That in youth ha'e spent in thee."*

Granted, he'd never studied her in that heated way, through thick-hooded lashes, singeing her with the intensity within their depths. But love was comfortable and kind, and…

59

Her fingers slid, creating a discordant, unharmonious cacophony, which ushered in more furious whispers.

"Away you thoughtless murd'ring gang..." Gemma's voice broke and wrenching her hands from the keyboard, she sprung from her seat. A tight, boulder-like pressure weighted her chest, squeezing off airflow. Her chest rose and fell in painful spurts as she looked to the silent, gawking crowd. Lord Westfield stared at her, with that blasted gentle smile. God, how that pitying look grated.

Yanking her focus from the marquess, her gaze collided with her mother, mouth agape. All the while, the other would-be future duchesses with their mean smiles and amused eyes no doubt reveled in this prolonged moment of humiliation. A panicky laugh bubbled up her throat. This miserable showing would knock her out of the proverbial running as a potential bride faster than one could utter "spinster forever".

With humiliation twisting her belly in knots, Gemma gave a toss of her nonexistent curls and took large, lurching strides toward the side of her chair. She marched past her row and quickened her pace. She continued walking until she reached the back of the hall. As she broke into a near sprint, the next flawless lady filled the hall with the appropriately perfect melody of *Der Wanderer*. German lyrics of which Gemma couldn't even make sense.

Fearing her mother would send Emery after her with the express purpose of dragging Gemma back to take part in another bloody song, she set off running through the duke's long, quiet corridors.

SEVEN

As Gemma continued her rapid flight, her heart beat loud and fast in her ears, thundering from the need to escape. To get away. To disappear from this stilted world of unkindness and inanity.

She skidded to a stop at the end of the hall and then studied the intersecting paths. Footsteps sounded behind her and her pulse kicked up a frantic beat that matched her ragged breathing. Gemma raced on down the hall to the double doors. Nearly suffocating from the oppressiveness of this whole affair, she shoved them open and stumbled out onto the moonlit terrace. With quaking fingers, she closed the massive oak panels behind her and leaned against the solid wood, taking support from it.

In a bid to blot out the humiliating shame forced upon her by her mother, Gemma closed her eyes tight. She concentrated on the symphony of crickets and night birds singing their nighttime song and allowed the soft summer air to caress her heated cheeks. A peaceful calm stole over her and she shoved away from the door and walked slowly down the length of the stone terrace. Gemma stopped at the edge of the balustrade and layered her palms upon the smooth Cast stone. She surveyed the stretch of country landscape bathed in the full moon's soft, white glow.

She'd long been an oddity; first among her family as the hopeless, socially awkward daughter and then when she'd been presented to Society. Words that came so freely and oft times eloquently with her family escaped her in the presence of strangers. Drawing in a breath of cleansing summer air, Gemma rested her forearms upon the ledge and leaned forward. She had not registered the true depth of her strangeness until she'd been thrust amongst the *ton*. Since that painfully awkward entry into Polite Society, she'd endured Season after Season, all to the same result—a continued marriage-less state.

She laid her cheek upon her arm. The truth was, she'd not truly minded waiting for the right gentleman. She'd never wanted a cold, emotionless union. She'd long dreamed of a gentleman who saw her as worthy; a man who appreciated her for her intelligence and celebrated her peculiarity. The rub of it was, she'd hoped with a naïve young lady's belief in happily-ever-afters that there existed such a gentleman.

Time had shown her but one. One gentleman who did not share her blood who waltzed with her. One gentleman who smiled and actually spoke to her, and not at her or about her. Yes, Lord Westfield had proven himself wholly unlike any of those others and he'd earned her heart for it.

So why should that smile he'd cast her way during the recital grate on her nerves?

Fighting a sigh, Gemma smoothed her palms over the stone balustrade. Because his was the pitying kind, is why. Never had the marquess stared at her with any real passion or desire in his eyes, but rather a benevolent warmth that she suddenly despised. Had it always been that way? Had she been so desperate for any kindness and the dream of love that she'd failed to note as much, until now? Until Richard.

The soft footfall of boots split her confounded musings and she spun about. Her heart skittered. As though she'd conjured him with a mere thought, Richard stood ten paces away with his hands clasped at his back. The moon cast a soft light upon his rugged features. She wetted her lips. "You."

He nodded once. "Me."

Which begged the question…"Why?" There was really no helping that, or her inexplicable ease around Richard Jonas.

Richard rocked back and forth on the balls of his feet and glanced past her at the countryside. "What if I said because I tired of the evening's entertainments?"

Gemma managed her first *real* smile that night. "Then I'd say we are remarkably similar in that regard." Yet, the more they spoke, the more alike she came to find they were in so *many* regards. She cleared her throat, uneasy with that revelation, and returned to her place at the balustrade. She looked down below to the ornate water fountains sculpted in the likeness of the Greek gods and goddesses of nature and harvest. From the hand of a chiseled Pan, water arced, glimmering in the moonlight and Gemma fixed on the soothing calm of the trickling water. "It was awful," she said softly.

The tread of Richard's footsteps indicated he'd moved. At his nearness, a thrill of awareness ran along her spine. When he remained silent, she shot a look over her shoulder.

"Yes," he said straightforwardly. "It was."

Most would be insulted at that blunt concurrence and, yet, she appreciated that honesty. She appreciated that he did not fill her ears with lies and platitudes. For her performance had been dreadful, as had been the entire experience this whole evening.

She started as he stopped beside her. How was it possible that a man of his sheer size and power should move with such a sleek grace and elegance? In a like manner to her own, Richard pressed his palms to the stone ledge. "You misunderstand me," he murmured. "It was dreadful but not in the way you are thinking."

Gemma creased her brow. "What other way *is* there to think of it?"

"Well," he said as he perched his hip on the ledge. He removed a flask inside his jacket and uncorked it. A frown formed on her lips as he drank from that flask, but his next words killed her intended chiding. "You, no doubt, referred to your performance." She warmed under his unerring accuracy. "Am I correct?" he prodded, winging an eyebrow up.

Gemma gave a slight nod.

"But all of this," he waved his flask over the countryside. "Is awful."

She eyed him perplexedly, as he tucked his drink inside his jacket pocket. "The duke's property?"

A smile hovered on his lips; those lips that had explored hers not once, but twice...and shamefully, lips she'd thought scandalously of in the privacy of her mind since. "The summer party arranged by the duke." Those lips twisted in a wry grin. "An event hosted with the sole purpose of marrying off his children. Then, there is the state of his health which quite explains why he wishes to see what is most important to him properly tied up, or in this case, married, before he dies."

Gemma tried to place herself into the duke's proverbial boots. She tried to imagine facing the end of her life and worrying over her children's marital state. Would she worry about witnessing a match made while she lived? Or would she wish that they know happiness and find love when fate decreed?

"Regardless, this is the way of our world. And so daughters are paraded before gentlemen who must see to their responsibilities after years of avoiding those very ones," she said unable to keep the regret from creeping into her tone. Suddenly, the frustration with a woman's lot in this stifled world boiled over and set her into a back and forth frantic pace. "Women are to fit within Society's stiff expectations and excel in each ladylike skill deemed worthy. Stitching—"

"Which I gather by your tone you're rubbish at?" he interrupted.

"Oh, quite," she said with an automaticity, never breaking stride. "The proper way to hold a fan." She made a show of holding an invisible hand and fluttering it before her face.

Richard swung his leg back and forth, elegant in his repose. "And I take it you have not perfected the art of using a fan?"

She sniffed. "Do I seem like the manner of lady who would perfect the art of using a fan?" She slashed her hand through the air. "No, my thoughts and knowledge of them are of the practical sort."

He rolled his shoulders. "Practical sort?"

"Ladies are expected to use them to signal a message to gentlemen," she said, coming to an abrupt stop so they faced one another. "But royal servants of Egyptians, they would use them for fanning insects and inciting flames to stir a fire." A mayfly landed on Gemma's cheek and she brushed it back, giving Richard a pointed look. "Do you see how a fan would be helpful for *this*? But no." She firmed her mouth. "Instead, the *ton* expects a lady to hold it to her mouth and send unspoken messages that can be interpreted one way by a gentleman where she really might mean an altogether different thing, and—" She let her breath out on a slow exhale as tension cloyed at her chest, threatening to suffocate her. Gemma searched Richard for signs of amusement.

She'd despise him if he made light of her. And yet, there was nothing but a stoic calm to his rugged features as he studied her. Faced with his silence, Gemma clasped her hands together and studied the interlocked digits. "But regardless, Society has their expectations of skills and attributes a lady should possess and, as such, it is ordained." Expected. Without an appreciation that not all women fit within the same proverbial mold of Societal perfection. That some ladies were invariably horrid singers, with clumsy fingers as it pertained to the pianoforte and embroidering. She sighed and drifted closer to the edge of the patio. "As such, it, as you indicated earlier, was awful. It, as in the recital and my singing." Gemma stared blankly out at the fountain of Diana and the water that spurted from the stone statue's arrows.

Richard reached a hand out and captured her chin between his thumb and forefinger. Her skin tingled from his touch. "The recital was awful, but you, Gemma Reed, were the one thing sincere about the whole event." His expression grew contemplative. "Perhaps, the sincerest thing about the duke's entire summer party."

Charged silence met that powerful declaration. Her breath froze and parting her lips, she looked up at him.

Richard dipped his head and a hint of brandy and honey caressed her lips. No gentleman had a right to that blend of scandalous and sweet upon his breath. Her lids fluttered and she leaned up on tiptoe—

The press of a door handle resonated like a shot in the night. Richard wrenched away with a quiet curse. In one fluid movement, he hefted himself over the edge, landing on his feet with a quiet thump of his boots.

She gasped and peered over the edge as he strode over to the duke's towering fountains.

"Miss Reed."

Heart racing, Gemma spun around. Lord Westfield stood at the end of the patio with a bemused expression on his face. "L-Lord Westfield," she squeaked. She fluttered her hand about her throat, expecting him to leave, and was further shocked as he pushed the door closed behind him.

Beatrice's brother stood contemplatively eying her the length of the expansive patio and then proceeded to walk toward her. Toward her. She gulped. Perhaps he was here to meet another. Gemma stole a glance about. After all, what was there to explain his appearance here, and…?

She leaned forward and searched for Richard. But he may as well have been a shadow swallowed by sunlight.

Lord Westfield cleared his throat, and she wheeled back. "I enjoyed your performance," he said softly, not taking his gaze from the stretch of countryside in the distance.

Gemma glanced around for the lady he spoke to, and…

He shifted his gaze to Gemma and she blinked. There were all manner of suitable replies she'd been schooled in by her mother, governess and nursemaids; the most obvious of which was "thank you". Instead, she blurted, "*My* performance?" A wry grin formed on her lips. "Did you refer to my singing or my flight from the recital hall?"

He favored her with a smile. "You have a lovely voice."

Either the Marquess of Westfield was stone-deaf or the kindest gentleman in the realm. She settled on the latter. So why did she appreciate the sincerity in Richard's earlier honesty? "Thank you," she forced herself to say when he continued to stare at her.

The marquess strolled closer and Gemma did a quick search about. If Richard was discovered here, she would be literally and figuratively ruined. The moon's glow rained down beside a towering replica of Michelangelo's David, spouting water, illuminating Richard behind that statue.

She rushed away from the edge of the balustrade and walked in the opposite direction, toward the crystal, floor-length windows lining the patio. Lord Westfield came to a stop. He took in her hasty movements through thick, golden lids. Gloriously blond lashes she'd long admired, that shielded the warmest, kindest eyes she'd known. Eyes that did not, however, smolder.

Not that she preferred a smolder. Smoldering was dangerous and she'd little interest in anything but a perfectly content, harmonious life built on happiness and love with the marquess.

An awkward pall of silence fell between them and Gemma searched her brain for something, anything, appropriate to discuss with this man she'd have as her husband. The words remained jumbled in her mind as they invariably always were around Lord Westfield and everyone. Everyone who was not Richard Jonas, it would seem. "A-are you not enjoying the evening's entertainments?" She stammered the insolent question that earned one of his patently charming smiles, revealing two rows of perfectly even, white teeth.

She tipped her head. It really was a glorious smile. With his tousled golden hair and easy grin, he had the look of the Lord's avenging angel, Michael. And how many times had this very man rescued her from misery during her London Seasons?

So why does my heart not race?

He inhaled the summer air and skimmed his gaze over the star-studded sky, and then leveled Gemma with his stare. "I watched your departure."

Her flight. There was hardly anything dignified or ladylike about her retreat. Gemma curled her toes. How long would this refrain of whispers go on from the other guests present? Unless there was another equally awful lady to follow, it would, no doubt, serve as a valuable source of gossip for the other guests present.

…The recital was awful, but you, Gemma Reed, were the one thing sincere about the whole event.

She wetted her lips and the marquess dropped his gaze, lingering on that slight movement. Heat slapped her cheeks. Oh, dear. In all her dreams, that was the precise hot stare she'd hoped for, but never expected from this very man. "S-singing, when one truly considers it, is a perfectly harmonious technique that requires the lungs, chest, tongue, and palate." Oh, bloody hell, now she'd gone and mentioned body parts. Again. And not in the natural way of discussing as it had been with Richard, but rather the inane ramblings of a lady wholly uncomfortable with the gentleman she'd admired for years. She gave her head a hard shake. *Loved. The gentleman she'd* loved *for years.* "Such a natural process, performed the same by all, and yet yielding such different results," she prattled. Inexplicably her gaze was drawn below and she adjusted her eyes in the dark to make out that statue concealing Richard Jonas' broad, powerful frame.

"But then how dull it would be if everyone yielded the same results." His breath fanned her cheek and she closed her eyes a long moment, willing the fluttering in her belly and rapid loss of senses. Remarkably unaffected, Gemma slowly opened her eyes. "I-I should—"

"You should not be cowed by Society, Miss Reed. You are kind where so many are cruel and there is something to be said of that."

She smiled. It was words such as those that set this gentleman apart from so many others. "Thank you," she said softly. But her heart still did not race. *Perhaps it is because I still do not know his kiss.* "I should be going." Gemma hesitated for a fraction of a moment; that pause borne of a need to know if Lord Westfield was so overcome with desire for her that he'd take her in his arms.

The consummate gentleman, he sketched a bow. Gemma took a step. When he spoke, his deep baritone brought her to a stop. "Will you take part in the archery display?"

Oh, it was assuredly a display. "I would not miss it, Lord Westfield." Where the other ladies present would be angling their bodies, using their bows as instruments to catch the marquess' attention, archery was the one ladylike endeavor she'd quite taken to as a girl. It was not a sport she used in a futile bid to capture a gentleman's regard.

The young marquess hooded his lashes. "I am glad," he murmured quietly.

Gemma called forth the butterflies and fluttering. Once more, that blasted enthusiasm escaped her. Gemma dropped another quick curtsy and hurried past him. And only when she'd made her escape and reached inside the duke's home with the door closed between them, did she search for a way to explain her relief at that parting.

EIGHT

T he following morning, Richard stood at the edge of the Duke
of Somerset's property. His mount, Warrior, lazily munched on
the thick brush. Sheltered by the thick copse of towering oaks and with
flask in hand, Richard purposefully worked his gaze over the lords and
ladies gathered on the well-manicured lawn.

In this next grand show for the guests invited to the duke's summer party, archers' targets had been set up. Various shaped bows in
their hands, ladies angled those respective instruments, using them to
show their figures off to advantage as they practiced taking aim upon
an imaginary target. One of the things he'd singularly loved about
Eloise had been her disinterest in the peerage. Oh, she'd gone on to
wed an earl but she had not melded with the world of Polite Society.
That had set her apart from all others. It made her unique...

He looked about for Gemma.

Or rather, it *had* made her unique. That was not the case, any
longer.

*...Women are paraded before noblemen. They are to fit within Society's stiff
expectations and excel in each ladylike skill deemed worthy...*

With her words flitting through his mind, Richard took another
drink. He settled his gaze briefly on Westfield at the center of the collected guests; the gentleman for whom Gemma intended to profess
her love.

Just a step below royalty, Westfield's coffers were vast enough to
rival a small kingdom. Yet, when such wealth made other men pompous prigs, Westfield was the manner of man who'd befriend a viscount's

younger son, and throw his loyalty and support behind him. A gentleman who'd leave a recital hall in search of a young lady who'd fled in embarrassment.

From their first meeting, he'd questioned the lady's motives where Westfield was concerned. Now, Richard acknowledged the truth: why should Gemma *not* love Westfield? The man was a bloody paragon.

He took another swill of his drink, absently studying a lady taking aim at the target and sending her arrow sailing. The distance muted the polite clapping, as the young woman stepped out of the way, allowing the next lady to come forward.

So why should it bother him that Westfield was a bloody paragon? Nay, it was not that Westfield was a paragon, but rather that Gemma Reed concurred and, as such, joined the fray of prancing, preening ladies.

The ghost of a smile pulled at his lips as he recalled her fluttering an imaginary fan before her face. Not that Gemma Reed would ever be one to fawn. There was such a raw honesty to the lady, missing in most of polite *ton*, that she was incapable of any such artifice. She was...

He squinted into the distance and did another sweep of the guests collected on the lawn.

Missing.

He frowned. Richard did another cursory look at the guests assembled. At the center of the bustling activity stood Westfield and, yet, even after her assurance to the contrary, the lady was conspicuously absent. Why would the lady seeking to cull the marquess' notice fail to take part? Not unlike her quick flight from the patio upon Westfield's appearance last evening, the lady did not seek to immerse herself in the fray of matchmaking.

From the corner of his eye, a flash of yellow fabric caught his notice. Richard froze and looked to the opposite end of the copse where...

He furrowed his brow.

Where...

Gemma stood surveying the guests assembled. She shifted something in her arm, revealing a flat bow. He slowly pocketed his flask and continued to study her furtive movements. What in blazes was the lady doing on the fringe of the morning amusements? Then, even with the distance between them, Richard noted the precise moment she locked her gaze on Westfield. Richard gritted his teeth. Westfield, the bloody paragon. Westfield…

Richard widened his eyes as she settled her bow on her shoulder. *Westfield the man she intended to shoot?*

With a silent curse, Richard sprinted through the copse. The lady glanced wide-eyed in his direction.

"Rich—"

He knocked into her slender frame and the abrupt movement sent her arrow flying through the air. As he took Gemma down, the bow tumbled to the ground beside them. "What are you doing?" he bit out against her ear. He opened his mouth to deliver a stinging diatribe upon her foolish ears when his body registered her soft, pliant form pressed to his. A surge of desire ran through him, blotting out words, obliterating rational thought, so all he felt and knew—was her.

Gemma stared wide-eyed up at him. Her chest moved quickly in a rhythm to match his own rapidly beating heart. "Richard," she whispered.

He really should be fixed on the madness in her letting loose an arrow at the man he'd called friend for over twenty years, except, his body responded to her nearness in form as he appreciated her in ways he'd not at their initial meeting; the gentle rise of her small breasts, the trimness of her waist, the delicate flare of her hips.

Gemma wiggled, shifting her hips.

His shaft leapt in response even as a pained groan lodged in his throat. In the distance, muffled cheers went up and that revelry had the same effect as a bucket full of frozen Thames water. He rolled off Gemma and jumped to his feet. "What in blazes are you doing?" he hissed. For it was far safer to focus on the lady's impulsive actions from moments earlier than his body's unwieldy response to hers.

"Beg pardon?" She shoved up onto her elbows and her loose chignon gave way under those efforts. The endless tresses cascaded about her back like a satiny waterfall. The sight of her sprawled on her back conjured all manner of wicked images, all involving those strands draped over his pillow and—

Richard closed his eyes and counted to five. He forced them open and found her eying him with her head tipped at that perplexed angle. "What did you think you were doing, aiming at Westfield?" With a quiet curse, Richard bent and scooped Gemma up. He set her on her feet and alternated his stare between the damning arch bow on the ground and the mad arrow-wielding lady.

Gemma rushed over and rescued the expertly crafted elm bow. Looking at the bow, she furrowed her brow. Then her eyes formed round moons. She jabbed an accusatory finger at him. "Never tell me you believed I was going to *shoot* the marquess?"

At the incredulity coating the inquiry, he yanked at the collar of his jacket. "I did not believe you intentionally sought to maim or wound," Or kill. "Westfield."

Gemma folded her arms at her chest, her possible weapon awkwardly jutted toward him, as she peered at him through suspicious eyes. "You think me incapable of shooting a bow," she said with a dawning understanding.

Another cry went up in the distance and Richard looked hopefully toward the far-off chatter. "If you are so eager to shoot a bow, I expect you are also eager to return to the activity planned by the duke."

Gemma remained with her booted feet planted to the ground and fixed an I-am-not-going-anywhere-until-you-reply-something-to-that-statement look.

Picking through his words carefully, Richard said, "I did not think..." She gave him a prodding, knowing look.

And he knew that look was intended to be more than faintly chiding and all he could note was the glimmer that set her eyes aglow in the summer sunlight. That gleam stole his thoughts, held him transfixed, until he no longer knew...

"I knew it," she muttered, cutting across the momentary blanket of madness she'd pulled over him. Then, in one fluid movement she grabbed up her arrow, positioned it within her bow, and with more than three hundred paces between the copse and the duke's party of guests, she took aim. Gemma let the arrow fly and it sailed unfailingly straight past the collective crowd of guests, gliding a hairsbreadth from Westfield's ear, and then finding its mark upon the center of the target.

"Bloody hell," Richard muttered. And as shocked gasps went up amongst the duke's guests, Richard launched himself at Gemma and took her down, once more. He brought their bodies in line with a towering oak.

She gasped. "What are you—?"

He glowered her into silence. "Unless you care to be discovered alone in my company," with nothing but ruin facing them, "by every last lord and lady gathered who are now trying to determine the whereabouts of the person who launched that goddamn arrow, then I suggest you remain quiet, madam," he said tightly against her ear.

The color leeched from her cream white cheeks. He clenched his jaw. He should hardly be offended that the lady was so loath to the possibility of being discovered with him. They were, after all, almost strangers, with her having marital aspirations trained on Westfield. So why did annoyance tighten his belly?

Thrusting aside the befuddled musings, he leaned his head around slightly. Ladies and gentlemen surveyed the area for the shooter of that mystery arrow.

"Was I seen?" she whispered and her warm breath fanned his cheek.

Once again, his body responded to her slender form flush against his. His mouth went dry…and he made the mistake of looking at her.

Healthy color now restored to her face, Gemma stared boldly at his mouth. Surely she was thinking of Westfield and the potential risk to her name. Should they be discovered, there would be no recourse for either of them, except marriage. The thought should bloody well terrify him. He'd long ago lost his heart to another; a young woman he'd called friend, whom he'd eventually come to crave more from.

But in all his imaginings of Eloise, his body had never felt—*this*.

"Why are you looking at me like that?" Gemma's whisper danced in the air between them.

Richard swallowed reflexively. "And how am I looking at you?" *As though I want to touch my lips to your flushed, heated skin and explore your body in every way, unlocking the secrets within.*

"As though I'm a plate of those kippers you so enjoy."

Or like that.

There should be humor at the likening. There should be amusement and, at the very least, a reminder of their innocent exchange in the breakfast room when they'd sparred and battled as almost enemies. "Ah, those kippers you so despise."

Gemma ran her gaze over his face "Do you know, Richard? I do believe you are correct." She wetted her lips and he followed that innocent, and yet wholly erotic, movement with his gaze. "I unfairly judged those kippers. I do not believe they are quite so horrible, after all."

He froze, as her meaning shifted into focus.

She reached between them and brushed a strand of hair behind his ear. "And I think those kippers will make someone a fine meal. *" Just not me...*

Of course, it wouldn't be Richard. Wordlessly, he looked off to the paragon in the distance. Eloise had chosen Lucien. Just as Gemma had chosen Westfield. As the second son of a viscount, Richard had never been, nor would he ever be, the man women chose to give their hearts to.

He stilled, suspended by the suffocating fear of his ponderings. He did not want Gemma Reed's love. She was nothing more than a woman he'd had but five exchanges with. Granted there had been two kisses there, as well. But still, five exchanges all the same.

Richard rolled onto his back, putting much needed space between them. Fishing around the front of his jacket he pulled out his flask and took a long swallow. A gentle breeze stirred the branches overhead and he stared at the dancing green leaves. "So why, Westfield?"

For a long moment, she said nothing, and he angled his head slightly, thinking she'd either failed to hear that inquiry, or ignored him.

Gemma lay on her back beside him, staring at the same canopy overhead. She chewed at her lower lip contemplatively.

"Beyond the terrier-like attributes," he said, infusing as much humor into that prodding as he could call forth.

She looked at him with a twinkle lighting her fathomless eyes. "I thought it was a hound?"

They shared a smile, but then his grin fell. "A dog is a dog." Just as certain men were rewarded with the love of a good lady. The Westfields and Luciens of the world. Both men, deserving of those very emotions and, as such, love found them.

Gemma shifted onto her side so she lay looking at him. "But that isn't true," she corrected. She propped her head on her hand. "Not even every terrier is the same. Redesdale terriers are vermin hunters and even-tempered. The Fox terrier," she waggled her eyebrows, "*also*, a terrier, mind you, but bred with a tempered aggressiveness to flesh out foxes."

He stared at her, bemused. "You know quite a lot about a lot of different topics, don't you, Gemma Reed?"

With a sound of frustration, she flopped onto her back beside him. "Much to my mother's chagrin," she muttered. "The *ton* hardly sees the benefit in a lady knowing anything about horses and dogs." And yet, even as Society favored a lady adept at the sport of archery, Gemma remained on the fringe, secretly participating in a way that wouldn't garner her notice.

Laughter filtered again in the distance, followed by the smattering of applause. Richard ignored it. For years, he'd admired but one woman, and that admiration had been built on a lifetime of friendship. He'd believed himself incapable of looking upon any woman, particularly one of noble origins, as different than the ladies in the distance vying for Westfield's hand.

Again, Richard looked at her. The walls he'd carefully built about a heart he'd thought forever numbed by Eloise's marriage to his brother, cracked.

As though feeling his gaze, Gemma turned and their gazes locked. "What is it?"

"You are a remarkable young woman," he said quietly.

And how had he failed to realize the lady's beauty at their first meeting? Except, he'd noted, and lying beside her, with her wide, brown eyes trained on his face, he had a staggering fear that now that he had noticed, he'd never stop.

NINE

Many words had been uttered about Gemma in the course of her life. Most of them beginning with the prefix "un": Unattractive. Untalented. Unimpressive.

Never, in all the words whispered about by the *ton*, or captured on the pages of the scandal sheets, had a single person penned remarkable beside her name. Not even the mother who'd given her life or the brother who loved her had seen her in that special light. Rather, she'd been recognized more as something of an oddity who would find love by sheer devotion.

Emotion swelled in Gemma's throat and she stared as the leaves danced overhead and revealed soft, white clouds as they rolled by. She turned her head. "No one has ever called me remarkable," she said softly to him.

A wry grin formed on his lips, but he didn't bother to take his eyes from the same clouds she'd previously studied. "Well, that is a near impossible feat. It would require a lot of unremarkable people to see something wholly absent inside themselves inside another." He spoke with a matter-of-factness that sent heat spiraling to her heart. Then he shoved himself onto his elbows and took another swill from his flask. Putting the top on, he stuffed it into the front of his jacket, and lay down on his back, once more.

Disappointment gripped her. Of course gentlemen drank spirits and, yet, his casual sipping from his flask, in that roguish manner, rankled. Rankled her, when it really wasn't her affair whether Lord Westfield's friend sipped spirits on Sunday with the devil himself. But she'd been so caught up in the beauty of Richard's words and now he'd dull that treasured moment...with liquor.

"So you never did tell me, Miss Reed," he said with that slightly mocking edge he'd used at their first meeting, bringing a frown to her lips. And *when* had she become Miss Reed, again? "What are the reasons you find yourself hopelessly in love with Lord Westfield?"

"Do you not believe him worthy of those sentiments?" she shot back.

"Quite the contrary. Though a rogue, Westfield is, as you said, loyal and kind. A better man than most of all Society."

She frowned. "Well, for one, he's not surly."

With their shoulders flush, her body trembled at the slight tensing of his bicep muscles. "Are you calling me surly, Miss Reed?"

"Are you calling me Miss Reed because you're being surly?"

He snorted. "Touché, Gemma. I wasn't always surly, you know." No, she didn't know. For she didn't truly know anything about Richard Jonas. Yet, at the same time, he knew more of her than any other. Even Lord Westfield...Unsettled by that truth, she fixed on the sound of his husky baritone. "In fact, I've been touted as one of those charming sorts."

She giggled. "Have you?"

In one smooth movement, Richard flipped on his side. "Not charming enough if that is any indication."

Her heart tripped a beat. Too charming if her pounding pulse was any indication.

She forced a smile. "And he smiles a good deal." At his silence, she asked, "Shall I continue?"

He inclined his head. "By all means." He dipped his lips close to her ear and slight shivers radiated at his nearness. "If you can, my lady."

If she could what? The muscles of her throat worked. "Er..." and she blinked several times, feeling as though he'd turned her in a hundred dizzying circles. "Of course I can." Of course she could what? *Think, Gemma Reed. Think.* Lord Westfield! Of course, they were speaking of Lord Westfield. Her future husband. Only, where her desire to capture that gentleman's notice had sustained her through three lonely Seasons, now, she struggled to draw forth his image.

Richard stared at her with a triumphant glimmer in eyes so gray they could rival a tempestuous summer storm. "Then please do con- tinue." What a hopelessly disloyal creature she'd proven—and all because of Richard's roguish half-grin. And his teasing. And his compliment that surely hadn't been intended as a compliment.

Think of all the ways in which Richard was *not* perfect. Her eyes snagged upon the front of his jacket. She stared damningly at it. "Well, he assuredly does not carry a flask in his pocket and drink with a staggering frequency."

He bristled. "I do not drink with a staggering frequency." Richard followed her stare. "Most gentleman do carry a flask," he mumbled under his breath.

Warming to all those needed reminders, Gemma went on. "Nor in all the years I've known him has he mocked his sister for her romantic tendencies and he certainly believes they exist."

A muscle jumped at the corner of his mouth. "I believe in love."

"You?" She rolled her eyes. "A gentleman who'd mock me for my words? Who in our handful of meetings has expressed cynicism for that sentiment? You don't believe in love, Richard, but it is real. It is…" Gemma trained her gaze on him, her words momentarily fleeing at his nearness. Heat poured from his thickly muscled chest and warmed her more than any summer sun could or ever would.

In a touch as fleeting as a butterfly's kiss, Richard ran his knuckles over her jaw. "For your opinions on me, Gemma, and your perceived thoughts on how I view love, you would be wrong."

She bit her lip and his eyes took in that slight movement, and for a heartbeat she thought he'd again kiss her. Thought it. Wanted it. Needed it—Then his words registered.

He spoke with a solemnity, devoid of cynicism that she'd not known of him these past days at the duke's summer party. "You speak as one who has known those sentiments," she ventured hesitantly, not knowing why it should matter if Richard Jonas had entrusted his heart to another.

"I have," he quietly confirmed.

And yet, it did. It mattered a great deal. A quiet silence fell between them with the revelry from the duke's arranged games forgotten.

"You have," she repeated blankly. He'd been in love. Or he still was.

Richard shifted his gaze and looked overhead and that slight distancing pulled at her heart. With that move away from her, he'd been drawn back to the lady who'd earned his love. She bit the inside of her lower lip, torn between asking questions that sought answers about who had hurt him and never wanting to know that there had been another...mayhap a woman who'd also known his kiss first. "I was in love."

Her heart missed a beat. *Was.* Not—am. "Is she the reason you carry that flask?" Hers was a bid to infuse levity back to their easier exchange, bringing them 'round to the safer discussion on those decorous traits one would expect of a gentleman.

He nodded. "I was not always cynical. I was very much in love."

Very much in love was so greatly different than just "in love". The regret in his tone spoke of a man who still cared deeply and Gemma ached to take that hurt away. For she knew what it was to care for another and to be very nearly invisible to that person. Abandoning all hint of hesitancy, Gemma flipped onto her side. "Why did you love her?"

He cocked his head.

Making a clearing noise with her throat, Gemma pushed herself up onto her elbow and looked at him. "Well, you see, I loved Lord Westfield because he so gallantly danced with me when no others would." *Or will.* She opened her mouth to continue but her breath caught as he rolled onto his side.

He brushed his thumb over her lower lip in a fleeting, too quickly ended caress. "Love."

Her mouth parted under his tender ministrations. "What?"

"Not you 'loved' him. Rather, you *love* him."

She formed a circle with her mouth. "Did I say 'loved'?" Surely she'd not make such a mistake. Surely, she'd at the very least recall making such a mistake?

His lips twitched. "You did."

"Humph," Bristling at his obvious amusement, Gemma frowned. "If I did say that, which—"

"You certainly did."

"Then, it was said in error," she spoke over him. "Regardless," she gave a flounce of her hair, never wishing more for a set of perfectly coiled ringlets than this very instant. "Why are you in love with..." She didn't want the lady's name, for it would make her real in ways that Gemma rather preferred her not to be. "Your lady," she finished. The muscles of her stomach knotted. Why should she care either way who Richard Jonas loved? Why, unless...?

"Why?"

For all the consternation in that one-word utterance, she may as well have asked him to deliver a lecture on the origins of life before the Royal Academy.

She stared expectantly at him.

"There is no one like her." That gruff reply came almost grudgingly. "She can fish and swim better than most gentlemen I know."

Again, Richard proved himself a man who desired more, wanted more, than the empty-headed debutantes flitting about London. Unlike the lords who craved a Diamond, he with his words proved himself one capable of appreciating a flawed, cracked, and more than slightly dulled diamond. It was on the tip of her tongue to add that she herself could no doubt best Richard himself in any lap across a lake. Not that she was competing with the nameless young woman he spoke of. She wasn't. Gemma chewed her lower lip. Well, mayhap a bit in her unspoken thoughts she was.

"Who was she?" The bald question slipped from her lips.

"She...*Eloise*, was a childhood friend."

Only, one would never be invisible with a childhood friend. Rather, that person he spoke of was a lady who'd know all the secrets he carried, and stories of his family, and all of him, really.

And Gemma really didn't wish to know anything more than that. For that lifelong connection spoke to more than a fleeting love that had come from a perfectly timed waltz, then quadrille, and pleasant exchanges at *ton* functions. Yet, he spoke in the past tense. "Was a—?"

"Is," he swiftly amended and hopped to his feet.

Pushing herself up onto her elbows, Gemma took in his restless movements. He flicked his gaze about the copse, his stare lingering in the direction of the distant amusements being enjoyed, concealed by the thick brush.

A private smile formed on his lips and it was as though he recalled memories only he knew of the lady. Envy snaked through Gemma. "She taught me to bait a fishing pole when I was a squeamish boy." He chuckled. "And she could curse and spit with an ease that would have impressed a hardened soldier."

Only one purpose had driven her efforts for this summer party; one man—Lord Westfield. That same gentleman now forgotten, Gemma climbed to her feet.

Tension dripped from Richard's tautly held frame. The hard glint in Richard's eyes spoke of a man who didn't care to discuss those parts of his past.

Selfishly, she wanted to know anyway. "What is she like now?"

He pierced her with his questioning gaze.

Gemma ran her palms down the front of her skirts. "Well, it is just the memories you speak of…" she picked her words cautiously, a near impossible feat given one so wholly inept when it came to Social discourse. "They are memories of your childhood. Who did she become as a woman?"

With a furious restlessness to his movements, Richard moved toward her. "Are you questioning whether or not my love for the lady is real?"

Unease raced along her spine at the volatile anger lighting his eyes. The gentleman was really not much more than a stranger and yet…she forcibly relaxed her shoulders. He'd not hurt her. "I am merely pointing out the memories you've shared, your reasons for loving her, they are borne from moments long ago. Who is she as a woman?"

He folded his arms in a defensive manner. "She is loyal, dedicated, devoted to her fam…" His words trailed to an abrupt end and a flush marred his harsh, angular cheeks.

Did he recognize the hypocrisy in spouting nearly the same words Gemma had so recently about Lord Westfield? "Forgive me," she said quietly. "It was not my reason to question your devotion to the young woman." She spoke in truth. Rather, her inquiries had been borne on an inherent need to know about what had shaped this man into the person he'd become. By his accounts, a man he'd only recently become. "What happened to her?"

Silence ticked on and she expected he'd not honor her with any additional answers about his past—and his love.

But then…

Richard lifted his shoulders up and down in a casual shrug. "She married another." A mirthless chuckle rumbled past his lips. "Two different someones, rather."

Two different…? Gemma creased her brow.

"Eloise left for London when she was eighteen and had her first Season." He gave his head a slight, sad shake. "I was too much a coward to confess my feelings for her."

"What happened to her?" she asked, the question tumbling out.

"She married an earl." A muscle leapt at the corner of his mouth. "A good man who left her a young widow."

That telltale tic gave her pause. Did Richard judge his own self-worth against those distinguished titles afforded a man for nothing more than his birthright? In truth, Gemma had never given a jot if a man was a duke or a driver; she judged their worth in the quality of their character. "And she remarried again after her husband's passing?" she put forward based on his earlier statement.

The foolish woman. Whoever she'd chosen could never be more devoted, more capable of melting a woman with his forbidden kiss than—

"My brother, Lucien," he finished.

She stared unblinking, while the birds chirped cheerfully from the branches overhead. His brother. The woman who won Richard's heart had wedded his brother. Emotion stuck in her throat. What must it be like to love a person, only to have them wed your sibling? The pain of that loss would be there forever; a reminder you could not escape. Just then, even with the inexplicable niggling of jealousy clawing at her, she was filled with something more—fury for the brother who'd so betrayed Richard. "I am sorry," she said lamely, shamed by her earlier flippancy. How futile those words must be to someone who'd loved so devotedly, only to be thrown over...for his brother.

Richard returned his gaze to her. A wry half-grin pulled at the right corner of his lips. "It would be easier if I hated them."

"But you do not," she said, taking a step closer. Gemma peered at him for a hint of all the emotion he kept beneath the surface of his roguish veneer.

"My brother is a good man," he said, a faintly defensive quality to his response. "He was forced into a commission by our father and went off to fight Boney's forces. He left behind a wife expecting their first child and returned only to lose his arm to infection and find his wife and son dead in his absence." The earlier fury burning through Gemma ebbed, leaving in its stead a wake of sadness for the brother he spoke of; a man who'd lost so very much and for that loss, was surely deserving of happiness.

Yet, that joy had come to him at Richard's expense.

Crossing over to him, Gemma came to a stop and hovered before him. Then, she quickly collected his hands in hers.

He started and dropped his gaze to their connected fingers. How greatly she'd judged the stranger with a flask in his pocket, hovering on the fringe of the duke's festivities. She'd looked upon the surface and prejudged him for supposed crimes against propriety and decorum. Humbled and shamed by that truth, Gemma gave his hand a slight squeeze. "I am so sorry," she whispered. Most other gentlemen would lash out at her, taking her words of the pitying sort.

His piercing, gray-eyed gaze remained locked on their joined hands. With the kisses shared between them, this touch was innocent in ways, and yet there was an intimacy to the connection that terrified. Gemma quickly pulled away.

Richard jammed his hands into his pockets and rocked forward on the balls of his feet. "I can regret that Eloise never loved me in the way I wished," he spoke with such a casualness of that lady's love that an odd wrenching pulled at her. "But I cannot begrudge her and Lucien their deserved happiness." With that, he proved the strength of his character and the goodness in his heart. When most would rail at the woman who'd chosen another, Richard spoke with a stoic acceptance and sad understanding for her decision. "To some, love finds its way. And to others…" Like him. "Well, the heart cannot help whom it loves," he said and nudged his chin in her direction. "Then, you know that, don't you, Gemma?"

Yes, she did. Or for three years, she'd thought she did. Now she no longer knew up from down. Drawn inextricably closer, Gemma drifted over to him so only a hairsbreadth of space separated them. The masculine sandalwood scent that clung to him floated about her senses, intoxicating. She trudged through the potent hold he'd cast over her and forced words out from a thick throat. "Do you believe yourself incapable of loving again?"

He hooded his lashes and brought a hand up to her cheek. His gentle caress set a wild fluttering inside her belly. "I believe love finds its way to those fortunate enough to desire it," he said gruffly.

Her lashes fluttered and she leaned up on tiptoe, needing to know his kiss again.

He dipped his gaze to her mouth. "Just as you found Westfield."

Those casual words spoken by Richard shattered her thick haze like a discordant violin in a silent ballroom. He stepped away from her and cast a deliberate look beyond her shoulder. Gemma whipped around.

Her heart started.

"It appears the day's entertainments are at an end," Richard murmured.

The afternoon's archery event now dissolved, Lord Westfield strode purposefully through the grass, to the sanctuary she'd stolen. A sanctuary she'd secured and shattered with one deliberate arrow.

Folding her arms at her waist, Gemma looked about the thick copse. There should be a sense of panic at being discovered with Richard, but there was a rightness, a comfortable ease between her and this man she'd known for but a handful of days. In his presence she felt none of the pressure to be something other than what she was. And there was a beauty to that and a need for the moment to stretch on to forever…

"Westfield is almost here. I will leave you." A tight smile marred his lips. "After all, I suspect your intentions with that arrow were to demonstrate your skill to that very gentleman."

A denial sprung to her lips, but then died a swift death. In this, Richard knew her better than she even knew herself. Her cheeks flamed hot. So where was the heady thrill at this stolen moment upon her with Lord Westfield?

With a sleek grace better suiting a stealthy panther, Richard retreated deep within the copse until Gemma remained, alone. Waiting with what should be breathless anticipation for Lord Westfield's arrival. Yet, there was a cloying panic and dread that made her tongue heavy and jumbled the words running in her mind so that she was the same uncertain lady bumbling through *ton* events. The snap of a branch brought her spinning.

Lord Westfield came to an abrupt stop. He flared his eyes, the blues radiating shock. Doing a quick sweep of the wooded area, his gaze fell to her flat bow and arrows. "Miss Reed," he said with no small degree of surprise in his words.

She shot a hand out and pressed her palm against the uneven oak, finding comfort in the solid, reassuring feel of it. "L-Lord Westfield." Her palms grew moist with nervousness and she prayed for even a hint of the excited fluttering roused by Richard.

Instead of bowing to propriety, the marquess strolled deeper into the thicket of tree and brush. He drew to a stop beside her archery equipment and sank onto his haunches. With a faint reverence he picked up one of her arrows and weighed it in his hand. "It was you."

Even as he spoke more to himself, Gemma nodded, anyway. "It was."

"I had to see who was responsible for that impressive aim and shot." Lord Westfield unfurled to his full length, impressive in his six-feet three-inches of masculine golden perfection. Yet, she remained oddly fixed on not the elegant figure he cut but rather Richard's earlier claim. Hers had been a rash bid to differentiate herself from that group of utterly perfect English ladies. To what end? She'd have a gentleman's regard for something more than an impressive showing with her bow. "What a remarkable shot, Gemma."

Gemma. Her fingers curled reflexively upon the ragged bark. Odd, how the use of her Christian name could so alter an exchange. "Th-thank you," she managed. For she really should say something.

A smile pulled at his lips as he strode ever closer.

The skin of her neck prickled and she fought the urge to search her gaze over the area. Was Richard here even now watching? What did he think of this stilted exchange? Did he feel even a frisson of the jealousy she had in his earlier telling of his lifelong love? She thrust away those foolish thoughts. Richard would not remain an interloper on this exchange, and especially not one which would threaten them both with discovery.

Lord Westfield stopped at the opposite side of the tree she still borrowed support from; that thick trunk all that separated them. He leaned slightly around and that slight movement allowed him an unobstructed view of her. "You did not care to join the day's entertainments?"

"I quite despise the triviality of these events," she said, giving him an honesty that, until now, had always come out stammering and rambling. Nay, until Richard.

"Yet you enjoy archery," Lord Westfield pointed out.

Gemma pushed away from the tree and did a small circle about the towering oak. "I enjoy it," she agreed. "But I enjoy the clearing as I rid my head of all thought and focus on nothing but the target calling my notice." Not the trivial display practiced by the other ladies earlier.

He eyed her bemusedly for a long moment and then he matched her movements. "You have intrigued me, Gemma."

The intimacy of his tone sent her toes curling reflexively into the soles of her boots, but she did not move away. For if she loved him, she should crave his words and his kiss with an equal fervor. How was she to truly know if he was her heart's truest desire if she continued to flee whenever he came near? "Then you would be the first," she said simply. With the same practicality she'd forged as a young lady venturing into the scientific study of horses and hounds, she eyed Lord Westfield curiously.

"Come," he made a sound of protest. "I do not believe that." He came closer, ever closer. "Surely there has been a gentleman not too much a fool to appreciate your uniqueness."

Richard's visage flitted through her mind. *You are a remarkable young woman...*He'd been the first to ever note anything about her, but his profession mattered for reasons so much more than that.

Beatrice's brother stared expectantly at her and she gave her head a clearing shake. She'd always been rubbish at this dance of words. Why could a man and woman not simply state their thoughts without this intricate stepping around what they truly thought, felt, or meant?

"I would wager, Gemma, that you are not at this summer party for the same reasons as the other ladies," he murmured.

A frisson of guilt ran through her. He would handily lose that wager. For her intentions were not unlike those other women, however, they were also vastly different. "I am not altogether certain how I am to reply to that," she said, pressing her palms together. *Tell him. Tell him how you feel. Tell him the words you've carried in your heart...*

Her lips went numb like a winter storm froze her from the inside, out. For did she truly love Robert, Lord Westfield? Richard, well, the woman he loved had been a young woman whom he'd known throughout his life, who'd shared a friendship, and who'd earned his heart. How very different than the three year, more stranger than anything, relationship she'd shared with her best friend's brother. The love Richard had for that woman had been borne of years of friendship, of special children's secrets, perhaps, and a lifelong bond forged early between them. What did Gemma truly have with Lord Westfield? Why, she didn't even refer to him by his Christian name.

"And that is what makes you different," he said, studying her the way he might a new genus of butterfly on display at the Royal Museum.

Her breath caught hard as he lowered his head. Where Richard had claimed her lips in an explosion that had left her breathless, Lord Westfield gave her time to pull away. Pressing her eyes closed, Gemma willed herself to feel, to turn herself over to his kiss and want him in ways that only a scandalous lady would.

He touched his lips to hers and she concentrated. They were firm and commanding and his breath bore the faintest hint of chocolate and brandy, an odd combination, and…She opened her eyes as he kissed her. And yet, she dissected his kiss the way she did a newly discovered piece of information. There was no explosion of simply feeling.

Gemma closed her eyes again as he angled his head, deepening that kiss, a meeting of their mouths which felt like a betrayal to another man.

I do not love him.

She went still and allowed that realization to creep in. Through the years, she'd loved the *idea* of him. In her darkest, loneliest moments amongst Polite Society, the dream of him coming to her rescue like a knight of old had sustained her through horrible, ugly, lonely balls and soirees. But in that, the Marquess of Westfield had never been anything more than the dream a lady might carry of romance and happily-ever-afters. Not truly. The whole of their meetings rolled together bore not a hint of the emotion or passion she'd known in four days with Richard. Gemma put her palms to his chest and a small groan escaped him. Taking a hasty step away, Gemma broke his kiss.

He blinked slowly. "Forgive me." A dull flush mottled his cheeks.

Another man, one with chestnut hair and teasing eyes, would never make apologies for having taken her in his arms. Gemma gave her head a pardoning shake. "There is nothing to apologize for," she said quietly. Then, as though scandal did not creep just outside the wooded copse, Gemma dropped a curtsy, picked up her bow and arrows, and then left.

As she made her hasty escape, she could not sort out which was worse; convincing herself she was in love with one man, while in truth, she'd lost parts of her heart to a man who'd only ever loved another.

TEN

From within his guest chambers, Richard stood at the edge of the floor-length window overlooking the duke's expansive, sprawling grounds. The moon bathed the earth in a soft, ethereal glow, a calming white light at odds with the inner tumult raging within him.

Reflected in the crystal windowpane, his flask sat mockingly on the side table beside his bed. With a handful of casual, direct words, Gemma, had upended his world. She'd forced him to look within himself, to the man he'd been, and the person he'd become in this past year. He didn't recognize the stranger from the respectable, focused gentleman he'd been.

Instead, he'd wallowed in the regret and pain of Eloise's marriage to his brother.

"...The memories you speak of, they are memories of your childhood. Who did she become as a woman...?"

Clasping his hands at his back, Richard passed a blank gaze over the countryside. He'd been indignant with Gemma's innocent questioning that morning. His sister-in-law Eloise was a good woman, for the devotion she'd shown to Richard's family in Lucien's absence. The truth was, Richard had exalted her to a status where she'd dwelt as a paragon of a woman. He'd seen no flaws. He'd marveled at her returning to the country to care for Richard's dying sister-in-law and nephew. When Lucien had retreated within himself after the war, Eloise had been the sole person who'd managed to draw him out, back into the living, and help heal their broken family. How could he not love such a woman? Only, in the silence of the midnight hour with nothing but his thoughts for company, he realized—he'd relegated her to the role of more saint than woman.

As Gemma had so innocently put to him: what had Richard's relationship been with Eloise through the years since she'd left for London almost ten years ago? She'd existed in frequent letters and the occasional visit, but he didn't truly know her beyond the memories shared from their childhood.

Odd, how he should know Gemma for but four days and yet he could close his eyes and breathe the honeysuckle scent that clung to her skin. He knew her interests, and admired her honesty, and her unfailing directness when all other ladies practiced prevarication the way they did every other ladylike charm. For what he knew, however, there was so much he did not. And he wanted to. The lady, in a few days' time, had battered down the cynical walls he'd erected about his heart and completely and hopelessly captivated him.

His mind danced around and then promptly shied away from what he truly felt for Miss Gemma Reed. "Get a grip on yourself, man," he muttered, pressing his palms into his eyes. He'd made more of their meetings than there was. Just because he could not rid his mind of the taste of her lips or the thought of her endearingly honest admissions did not mean he felt anything where the lady was concerned.

Except, thoughts of Westfield taking her mouth in a kiss slowly trickled in like an insidious poison, invading every chamber of Richard's mind. It spread out, numbing so that the muscles of his stomach clenched. And this blinding rage did not feel like nothing. It felt very much like—*something*, something potent, powerful and so very different than the dull regret he'd known with Eloise's marriage to Lucien.

Abandoning all hope of sleep, Richard made a disgusted sound. He stalked over to the door and wrenched it open. With purposeful strides, he strode through the duke's quiet home. At the late night hour, the guests occupying the chambers were silent in their slumbers. He tightened his jaw. Only Richard remained haunted by the complexity of his midnight musings. He scoffed. Why, even the lady who'd laid siege to his thoughts was no doubt tucked firmly under the covers of her soft, down bed, and…

An agonized groan stuck painfully in his chest as his supposition carried him down a path that involved the spirited Gemma Reed sprawled on satin sheets with her brown tresses cascading about them in a shimmery curtain.

Richard turned at the end of the corridor and, keeping his gaze forward, marched down the steps, and continued on to the billiards room. For perhaps with the world asleep around him, he could seek out the answers to whatever this was, in that room where she'd professed her love to…he shoved the door open and stepped inside.

Westfield.

The other man sat slumped in his seat with his head buried in his hands. Richard's sudden appearance brought his friend's head up, and Westfield stared back at him through tired eyes. How many times with his father's wasting illness and eventual death had he bore the same defeated, agonized expression in his eyes? "Jonas," Westfield greeted and made to rise, but Richard waved him to a sit.

"Forgive me," he said, a flush burning his neck. "I did not mean to interrupt." He turned to go, not wanting to sit casually across from this gentleman who'd long been a friend but now a man who'd kissed Gemma's lips.

"Stay, please," his friend said tiredly and climbed to his feet.

A protest formed on his lips but then he saw the demons haunting the marquess' eyes and, reluctantly, Richard closed the door behind him.

"A game of billiards?" Westfield asked. Before Richard could formulate a reply, the other man marched to the rack on the wall and removed two sticks. Born to one of the oldest, most respected titles in the realm, Westfield oftentimes demonstrated the power of that role; where a question was more a command.

Richard hesitated and then made his way to the table. The marquess turned over a cue stick. "Two hundred points?"

He made to speak. Except, he stared at Westfield's lips as they moved and Richard's fingers curled hard around his cue stick. He thought of those lips on Gemma's, claiming them as Richard had. Had she moaned with the same breathless desire? A long, slow growl climbed up his chest and lodged in his throat.

Furious energy thrummed inside him. How very casual Westfield was taking a position alongside Richard. The man spoke of billiards and points, while all the while Richard tortured himself with the earlier embrace he'd had no right to witness. Wordlessly, they let their cues fly at the same time.

"Your shot," he said gruffly as Westfield's ball rested closest to the baulk cushion.

A thick silence descended. With an unsuspecting Westfield examining his shot, Richard studied the other man. He'd known the Marquess of Westfield for more than twenty years. In the course of their friendship, the other man had proven loyal, unwavering, un-pompous, and more brother than friend.

It spoke a good deal about the manner of lousy friend and dishonorable bastard *Richard* was. For playing billiards, with Westfield casually eying his shot, he wanted to knock the other man on his bloody arse. And it also forced him into a moment to confront the irrational, but now obvious, truth.

I want Gemma.

He slid his eyes closed a moment. He wanted her in all the ways a man could know a woman. With her clever wit, unapologetic honesty, and endearing ability to tease, she was the lady he'd spend the rest of his life with. A strangled laugh clogged his throat. The great irony of this moment did not escape him. Gemma, a woman who'd never want anything more with him, had shown him the truth of his feelings for Eloise, opening his eyes to nothing more than the lifelong friendship that had existed.

In the quiet of the room, he studied Westfield as the other man walked a bored path around the red baize table, hating him, even as he had no right. Hating him for having secured the affections of a woman who was real and honest and who, for those reasons, would make him a bloody perfect duchess. "Are you going to take your goddamn shot?" he snapped.

His friend blinked several times and then glanced about. He furrowed his brow in abject confusion. Not unlike the way he'd blinked like a besotted sop when Gemma had broken the kiss.

"I said are you going to take your goddamn shot." Yes, he wanted to do more than knock Westfield on his arse. He wanted to knock him bloody senseless.

"You are in a rotted temper," the other man said with a slight frown.

That slight rebuke gave Richard pause and he silently cursed. He tossed aside his stick and crossed over to the sideboard. Where once, avoiding Eloise and Lucien's presence had seemed tantamount to his sanity, now remaining at the duke's goddamn matchmaking summer party threatened his very survival. "Forgive me," he mumbled. He picked up the nearest crystal decanter and then froze.

…He assuredly does not carry a flask in his pocket and drink with a staggering frequency…

With another growl, Richard slammed the bottle down hard. Drink with a staggering frequency, did he?

I carry a goddamn flask in my pocket.

"I say, Jonas, are you all right?"

"Fine," he bit out, ignoring the concern underscoring his friend's tone. "Fine," he forced himself to say again. "I am just…" Except, by God he didn't know just what he was. All he knew was that in just a handful of days, Gemma Reed had made him question everything he'd carried in his heart. First, she'd challenged his regard for Eloise; innocently remarking on his musings from long, long ago, and not borne of the now.

Then she'd bloody well kissed Westfield. Another snarl hovered on his lips and he tamped down the unfair expression. "Forgive me." He forced the tension away and returned reluctantly to the side of the pool table, just as the other man took his shot. The crack of Westfield's cue ball hitting his red target echoed in the room and snapped Richard from whatever maddening haze Gemma Reed had cast.

Guilt crept steadily in, driving back his irrational jealousy. Westfield's father was at the end of his life, suffering not unlike Richard's own father had years earlier. What did it say about Richard that he'd begrudge the other man any happiness—even if it was in Gemma's arms?

"Have you selected a bride from the guests assembled?" He didn't realize he held his breath until Westfield spoke.

"Hardly," he mumbled. "My father would have me wed Lady Diana Verney." He grimaced. "Not even eighteen years of age, but entirely *suitable* given her father's connection to mine."

Of course. A fellow duke's daughter, the lady was proper, pretty, and polite. The manner of young woman who would never bumble her way endearingly through a song or sneak about her host's country estate to boldly declare her love. "She would make you a perfect bride." As soon as the words left him, Richard realized the depth of the bastard he was. He'd encourage Westfield's suit with that woman for entirely selfish reasons. "That is, unless there is another lady who's earned your regard?"

"None," Westfield muttered. "I'm not fool enough to give my heart a second time." He took a sip of his drink.

None was the perfect answer. Or it should be for what it signified. Gemma's regard was unreturned. There should be a selfish elation at that discovery. So why did thinking of Gemma professing her feelings to Westfield only to be rebuffed cause this dull throbbing in his chest? Because he knew the pain of that rejection and would spare her from that, even if it was at the expense of his own happiness.

"Come," he said gruffly. "Surely there is one lady who has earned your favor?" He pressed. Not just for Gemma, but also for Westfield who deserved more than the flawless Lady Diana.

The marquess froze, bent over the table, examining his next shot. "There is one," he said under his breath.

Richard's heart slowed to a stop. Perhaps there was another young lady. Perhaps it was someone who would bring happiness to Westfield, and...He curled his hands into fists. But then, that would also mean Gemma's misery. "Oh?" He infused as much boredom as he could into that single syllable utterance.

"Miss Gemma Reed." He let his stick fly and then gave a pleased nod as he struck his intended target. A dry grin formed on his lips. "She is not what I'd consider a beauty by any stretch of the imagination."

Rage twisted and turned inside Richard. Now, he wanted to hit the other man for entirely different reasons. *Didn't you, at your first meeting, see Gemma as a dull, unmemorable figure?* He again briefly closed his eyes. How had he not realized the depth of her dark beauty from the start?

Westfield looked over the top of his snifter at him. "Do you know the lady?" Richard managed a movement that was not quite a shake and not quite a nod. "There is something intriguing about her."

And Richard really didn't wish to know any more. Nausea settled like a pebble in his belly. "Is there?" How did he manage to force out those words? Only, he already knew the answer—there was everything intriguing about the young lady. "Enough that you'd offer her marriage?" The muscles of his stomach clenched reflexively.

"I haven't yet decided." Some of the tension eased. Then…"I may." That was it. Those were two simple words. But those words were inconclusive affirmation, which really should matter not at all. So how did he explain the pressure tightening his chest? With a casualness that set Richard's teeth on edge, the marquess cracked his knuckles. "Then, if I must marry someone, I might as well spend my days with someone, at the very least, interesting."

His patience snapped. "Did you ever stop to consider that the lady deserves more from a husband than that?"

A knife could cut the thick tension in the room. Lord Westfield puzzled his brow.

An awkward pall fell over the room as Richard stood there clenching and unclenching his fists.

Yet…

It was what Westfield *possibly* wanted. And it was what Gemma absolutely wanted.

It just also happened to be what Richard detested to his core. "Indeed, you are correct, though," he said half-heartedly, his tone hollow to his own ears. His ears burning, Richard randomly thrust his cue. His shot went wide. "I am leaving tomorrow," he said sharply and abruptly set his stick on the edge of the table. He could not remain here any longer. Not when it would mean self-torture at the inevitable joining of Gemma with his closest friend. "I am not myself at these affairs." Or any *ton* events. Nor had Richard ever enjoyed, welcomed, or reveled in the inanity of the affairs. He enjoyed them a good deal less when he had to consider witnessing the future Duke of Somerset's courtship of Gemma Reed.

Westfield frowned. "I understand there are places you'd rather be than at a matchmaking party assembled by my father," Westfield said, returning his attention to his cue ball. "If I could leave, I certainly would. But," he thrust his stick forward, "never tell me you intend to leave on the morn?" Consternation rang in his friend's words.

Confirmation rested on Richard's lips. Except the moment he left, all he'd shared with Gemma would cease to be. The next time he'd see her would, no doubt, be on the arm of Westfield, either married or betrothed. "I will stay through to tomorrow's entertainments." Partially because he was a glutton for self-torture, but more, because he'd see her one more time before he rode off and left her to her heart's *greatest yearning*. Bile climbed up his throat and threatened to choke him. This was so much worse than anything he'd ever known with Eloise's decision to wed his brother. This was a rusted blade of jealousy raking his skin. This was burning regret and ugly resentment. It turned him into a person he detested. "If you'll excuse me?" He sketched a short bow. "I am going to seek out my rooms." Not allowing Westfield to waylay his efforts, he marched from the room.

ELEVEN

The lit chandeliers in the Duke of Somerset's ballroom doused the room in artificial light cast by thousands of glowing candles. Shadows danced upon the gold, satin wallpaper.

From her vantage at the corner of the ballroom, Gemma trailed her fingertips along the smooth, soft, cool to the touch surface. All the while, she eyed the gathering of guests. Charged excitement layered the air. Eager matchmaking mamas and their desperate-to-wed-a-duke daughters flicked frantic gazes about the room in search of the respective gentleman.

Unbidden, her gaze sought out Mama who stood speaking with another one of the distinguished mamas gathered, pretending to pay attention. All the while, she shifted her stare about the ballroom. Shame curled Gemma's toes. For, as much as she loved her mother, and as much as she knew her mother loved her in return, it was a painful moment to realize that her last living parent was not unlike the other grasping guests present.

"I always suspected you were a wallflower by choice."

She gasped as her brother's gently spoken words brought her around. Drat. She'd been discovered. Slamming a hand to her breast, she pasted a smile on. "Emery."

The orchestra struck up the next set—a quadrille and she welcomed the distraction of their enthusiastic playing. Her brother sipped from his champagne. "I am surprised."

He dangled that like bait. As someone who'd risen to far too many of those lures through the years, she recognized it, just as he knew that she could not indulge him. "What are you surprised at?"

Crystal flute in hand, Emery gave a slight wave. "That after all these years of pining for Westfield, and the sea of vultures descending upon him, that you'd not find the gumption to tell him."

She blinked and then searched about for possible interlopers. Alas, the collected guests would have to note the ever-ordinary Gemma hovering behind the great Doric column. *"...You are a remarkable young woman..."*

"Hmm? Nothing to say?" At her brother's pointed look, she dragged forward a suitable reply relevant to his mention of the marquess. For as much as Emery saw, or rather, as much as he thought he saw, he could not know, even now, another occupied her thoughts, that Richard Jonas had stolen her heart. The air left her on a slow exhale. *I love him.* She slid her eyes closed. All these years, she'd hung on to the dream of one man, only to find the reality of Richard Jonas so much more meaningful, in ways that stirred equal parts wonder and terror in her breast.

"Gemma?" The concerned question in her brother's tone brought her eyes open.

"This is hardly the place to speak on it," she said at last, owing her brother some response. She made a show of studying the partners circling in the steps of the quadrille. All the while, panic built inside, threatening to consume her. With a rapidity that defied the logic she'd long prided herself on, Gemma had gone and fallen in love with a man who loved another. How could she *ever* compete with the unattainable paragon that Richard had known for the better part of his life?

"So you'll not deny your feelings for the man?"

Trapped.

She sighed. He'd always managed the upper hand. But then, wasn't that the way of elder brothers? Promptly snapping her lips into an uncooperative line, Gemma peeked around the pillar.

"There are certainly worse gentlemen you could find yourself married to," he spoke in such hushed tones she strained to hear. "He is a rogue but he is not a rake. He is a loyal son and brother. And, of course, he possesses one of the fattest purses in the kingdom."

She shot him a frown. Did he think she was the manner of lady who desired material wealth?

"Not that you require a fat purse," he said quickly.

That was the manner of man Lord Westfield was. As Emery said, a good son and brother, yet for her brother's observations about that distinguished lord, she could not help but feel…empty at the prospect of life with the marquess. Her brother enumerated all Lord Westfield's outstanding attributes and, yet, his perfunctory list felt more an indictment against the gentleman than anything.

A commotion at the front of the ballroom called the crowd's attention and a buzz of loud whispers echoed from the walls. Absently, Gemma looked to the front of the room. The orchestra drew the lively quadrille to a rousing finish and absolute silence met the future Duke of Somerset's arrival.

He had arrived.

Lord Westfield stood at the top of the stairwell. Beatrice on his arm, he eyed the ballroom like a medieval knight upon his dais surveying his people. Then, these were his people. These were the lords and ladies called together by a dying duke with the express intention of marrying off his children. The marquess made his way down the marble staircase and said something to his sister that earned a laugh.

"You disapprove of the marquess?" she ventured hesitantly, pulling her focus away from Lord Westfield.

There should be something affirming in having all her own thoughts these years about that very gentleman carefully echoed by her brother. Yet, what would he say to the truth that she'd gone and fallen in love with another? A man who'd seared her lips forever with the memory of his kiss.

"Do you know what, Gemma?"

Pulled to the moment, Gemma silently shook her head.

"He will make any lady a perfectly fine husband, but you are not any lady." He downed the contents of his glass and dangled the empty flute between his fingers. "You are my sister. And I would have you with a gentleman who notices you and not a rogue who takes three years to see that you are there, Gemma."

Her throat worked and she leaned up on tiptoe. Emery stiffened as she placed a kiss on his cheek. "Thank you."

Cheeks flushed, Emery waved his empty glass. "Yes, well," he said, giving his throat a clear. "I am going to seek out the card rooms." He waggled his eyebrows. "Because that is the manner of gentleman *I* am."

A laugh bubbled from her lips and she swatted him. "Go." She stared at his swiftly retreating form. He moved with the speed of a man who'd been granted the king's pardon. There was no more loving brother and, yet, he'd never been one for those shows of emotion. Which is why his words resonated.

Her smile faded. Emery spoke of her finding a man who'd noticed her and, yet, Richard, who'd swiftly captured her heart, had noticed another and for it, he would only and forever see that woman. Gemma could not compete with the illustrious figure he'd held aloft. *I want to, though. I want him to see me…and only me…*

Just as her brother had said. After years of being invisible to every single lord at every infernal ball and soiree, she wanted to be appreciated and noticed for who she was. And Richard was the man to give the lady who owned his heart that strident devotion. Alas, there had been another before her. A faceless woman Gemma could have never hoped to compete with for Richard's sheer connection to that lady.

She stilled. Her skin burned with the feel of being watched. She did a sweep and found him. Richard stood at the pillar on the opposite end of the ballroom, staring at her with a burning intensity. And this was not a man who did not notice her. This was a man who, even with the distance separating them, pierced her with the heat of his stare, stirring a wild fluttering inside her belly.

Gemma cocked her head. Or rather, she thought he was staring at her. She peeked around, looking about for the other person who might have secured his focus. Looking back to Richard, she found him smiling—very much, at her. Nor was his the jaded, cynical grin, or the cocksure half-grin she'd come to expect. This was a sincere expression captured in honesty. She returned his smile. She cast a furtive look about, looked back and lifted her hand in a faint greeting.

Richard held his fingers up.

There was such an intimacy to their stolen exchange that felt more scandalous, more intimate, than any of the bolder, more passionate embraces they'd shared. Her heart doubled its beat. And for a gentleman who'd only seen one woman, and pined for her enough to carry that flask, he stared at her...as though there was only Gemma. Then, with a single-minded purpose, he walked the perimeter of the ballroom. Occasionally the kaleidoscope of twirling dancers separated them and with each step that brought him closer, a breathless anticipation filled her.

Gemma pressed her warm palms against the smooth column, feeling nothing but the thrumming energy inside. Two years earlier, she'd attended a lecture at the Royal Academy. On display had been the Leyden jar which kept electricity contained inside. With lords and a smattering of ladies yawning about her, Gemma had perched on the edge of her chair, transfixed by that clear, crystal container. How was it possible for energy to be so contained? As energy thrummed inside her—she knew.

Her heart thumped as he continued his forward path, his powerful stare not leaving hers. It was odd how even separated by more than thirty paces with a crowd of guests between her and another being, she could feel by the fix of his eyes and the sweep of his lashes that mesmeric connection.

Then Lord Westfield stepped into his path and the magical pull died a jarring death.

As Richard slowed to a stop, he slid his attention from Gemma to the future Duke of Somerset. From her cover behind the pillar, Gemma's heart sank. She hovered in her hiding spot. With her blatant attention, she was not unlike every lady present now eying those two converging gentlemen. Except, where so many of the others studied one with a single-minded purpose, Gemma fixed on the other. She'd not been unlike those other ladies; raising the Marquess of Westfield to an illustrious status, seeing a paragon and not a man. Not unlike the way Richard had elevated his Eloise to a lofty status to which no woman could dare aspire.

Now, with the two gentlemen side by side, she could not help but compare them. One gentleman, who by his birthright had been born to near royalty, and the other, who found himself born a second son and who'd subsequently built an existence with his skill and intelligence. That was the manner of man she'd spend her life with.

The two men sketched bows and then moved in opposite directions. Lord Westfield did a quick sweep of the room, but she looked away, instead seeking Richard. She wrinkled her nose. Blast and blazes. Where was he?

"Miss Reed, we meet again," Richard's voice sounded over her shoulder and with a gasp, she spun about.

"Mr. Jonas," she whispered. Of their own will, her eyes caressed the increasingly familiar planes of his harshly beautiful face. How singularly odd. To have come to the duke's summer party with one intention, only to find her world so singularly upended in just five days. It defied the logic, reason, and sense she'd lived her life by. It made a mockery of time and, instead, presented her with a new, unfamiliar, and yet thrilling aspect on life—and love.

In three years, she could place on her fingers and toes the number of sets a gentleman had sought from her. That was, not coerced by her protective and loving older brother. *Ask me to dance. Ask it because you wish it…*

And suddenly, she who'd hovered on the fringe, awaiting a gentleman to show some proverbial interest to her because he'd been so moved, tired of it, at last. "Do you dance, Richard?"

He furrowed his noble brow.

"Dance," she said slowly, motioning to the dancers now taking to the floor for the next set.

Confusion receded and Richard winked. That slight, seductive movement set off another round of fluttering in her belly. "Do you think because I breed horses that I'm unable to dance a waltz?" There was a dry teasing to that inquiry and, yet, layered within that question, hinted a vulnerability that came from his birthright as spare to an heir.

How could he not fully know a man was defined by more than his title, but by his strength of character and wisdom?

"No." Leaning up on tiptoe, Gemma shrunk the distance between them. "I believe because you haven't asked me to partner you that you're unable to dance."

By God, the lady had shamelessly challenged him.

Nay...

Holding her bold-eyed stare twinkling with mischief and merriment, Gemma Reed had done something more. She'd, in a roundabout way, asked him to dance. At her uncompromising commitment to saying the words she wished to speak and not cowing to Society's strictures, she rose all the more in his estimation. His throat worked as he accepted that safe description of how the young woman had buffeted his world.

At his continued silence, she waggled her eyebrows in a teasing manner. "Well?"

He could easily make light of her question and present an equally teasing response. He could make his excuses and turn on his heel and run as far and fast as was safe. And given his friend's revelation last evening of his intention to ask for Gemma's hand, well, if Richard was at all honorable, he'd reject the unspoken request.

But he was a bastard and a miserable excuse of a friend.

Wordlessly, Richard extended his elbow and Gemma automatically placed her fingertips on his sleeve and allowed him to guide her from the tucked away corner she'd found herself this evening. "So tell me, Gemma," he began as they took their places among the other dancers. "Do you make it a habit of lingering on the sidelines?" First the copse and now the edge of the ballroom.

She lifted her hand to his shoulder and he placed his at her trim waist. "Yes." A surge of heat burned through her satin gown, singeing his gloved hand, and he ached to yank the glove off so that small barrier between them was gone.

"Yes, what?" His voice emerged a garbled cough.

With a maddening, but equally sobering, nonchalance, Gemma rolled her eyes. "Yes, I do prefer to hover on the fringe." As he set them into motion, twirling her in the meticulous, requisite circles, Gemma nibbled her lip. A contemplative glimmer glinted in her brown eyes. "I've never craved, nor desired, to be noticed by Society."

Yet, with her marriage to Westfield and her ascension to the role of duchess, she'd be vaulted forevermore into the realm of Society's notice. That statement of truth hovered on his lips. To utter that deterrent to her quest for Westfield's hand would be the height of selfishness. He was a bastard. He was not, however, that much of a selfish bastard.

So instead, he asked a question that only deepened this useless bond between them. "What do you crave?"

At his soft whispered words, her slender body tensed in his arms. She raised stricken eyes to his. "No one has ever asked me that."

His fingers curled reflexively about her waist and her full lips trembled apart. "Then, that is a great travesty, Gemma Reed." And there in the midst of the ballroom of his best friend's home, and Society surrounding them, Richard dipped his head. "Because you matter," he said gruffly. "You matter more than the match you might make or the approval of Society. You matter because you are a woman so wholly different than any other," *I've known.* "Here," he stumbled over that word. Only, she was so very much unlike any he'd ever known. Even Eloise.

A shuddery gasp slipped out and floated to his ears. It was that faintly breathless admission that said nothing and everything, all at the same time. The most significant in that moment being that he was going to hell for wanting her as he did.

The long, graceful column of her throat moved. "I want to be loved," she said on a tremulous whisper and he went taut. "I want to be loved for who I am by a gentleman who has no desire to change me." Only a fool would attempt that useless feat. "I want to be with a man who will speak with me about things that matter and who won't expect me to be nothing more than a pretty arm ornament."

I could give you all that.

And he would have. If he'd but seen her first. Richard worked his gaze over her face. If he'd been the gentleman three years ago to attend that same blasted ball Westfield had and instead of the marquess rescuing her, it would have been Richard there. Then what would this moment be even now?

But it could not have been him. Because three years ago, he'd pined for the dream of a woman who was never meant to be—not for him. For that useless absorption in another, he'd failed to enter the living and see who was before him.

"You deserve that, Gemma Reed," he said solemnly. "And I have no doubt you will know that love with a deserving man." He spoke with a matter-of-fact truth that came from a genuine knowing. Westfield would care for her, and respect her, and not stifle her the way most of the mindless dandies scattered around this very ballroom would.

Gemma opened her mouth, but no words came out. She closed it and then opened it again. "I would speak to you. Alone." As soon as the scandalous admission left her mouth, her face exploded in color.

His muscles went taut. "Regarding West...what brought you to Somerset," he swiftly amended. Oh, God, she'd enlist his support with Westfield. If it weren't cutting him open inside, he would be laughing at the comedy of errors his life had become in five days.

She hesitated and nibbled at her lower lip. "Yes. It is about Westfield."

"Westfield," he repeated dumbly. At his audible utterance, Gemma stole a frantic look about.

"Yes." A wave of coldness invaded every corner of his being, chilling him from the inside out. When Eloise had chosen first an earl and then, after that gentleman's passing, Richard's own brother, over Richard, there had been a melancholy regret. For what could have been, but would never be. How could Gemma's disregard cut to the quick so that he could not even string together two rational thoughts to form a sentence. "In a way," she swiftly added. "I thought as we'd become...friends, that you would honor me that meeting."

Friends. "I see," he said flatly. So they'd moved from needling strangers, to passionate embracers, to...friends. No doubt she wished to ask questions about Westfield and ways that she might win the gentleman's favor. His lips twisted in a pained grimace. Of course, she could not know that with a too-quick, but not erroneous decision, the marquess had already settled on her for his future duchess. A growl stirred in his chest, until he wanted to toss his head and spit and snarl like an enraged beast. Bloody hell, he wanted so much more. By the prodding in Gemma's eyes, she expected him to say something and, coward that he was, he wanted to escape. "Meeting in private," any more than they had, "would not be prudent," he managed. It was a desperate appeal to the fates to kill a private meeting that entailed her singing the deserved praises of Westfield. For that was vastly safer and preferable than uttering the truth.

Of course, he should know a woman of her courage and determination would not be swayed. "There are some who are worth braving all for."

Her words drained the breath from his lungs, leaving his chest frozen. By God, she was right. Some were most assuredly worth braving all for. He'd spent the better part of his life burying his own feelings deep. She deserved more than to be settled on. Westfield had three bloody years to see Gemma Reed before him and he'd failed. Seeing others as more worthy than himself, he'd, not unlike Gemma, stood on the sidelines of life. And if he let her do this thing, if he waited for Westfield to decide whether she was "suitable" for his future bride, then Richard would spend the rest of his life hating himself for not having the courage to at least tell her what was in his own heart. It would be a life of constant wondering and regret. "You are correct," he said quietly.

She peeked about and then lowered her voice all the more. "But it cannot be here, Richard." The orchestra drew the dance to a slow stop and Richard had never been more mournful and more grateful for the sudden conclusion of a dance. They stood at the side of the ballroom with rapidly departing couples moving all around them. "Will you meet me in the duke's library after the next set?"

TWELVE

For a long moment, Richard said nothing. And for an even longer, more horrifying moment, she expected he'd refuse. It was as he said. If they were discovered or overheard, she would be ruined. And yet, there were surely worse things than being ruined. Never telling the gentleman who'd shown her the wish she'd never known she carried in her heart, that she loved him. That was far worse. Unease roiling in her belly, Gemma fidgeted with the card at her wrist, momentarily bringing Richard's attention there.

Then he gave a brusque nod. "Of course."

Her shoulders sagged in involuntarily relief and she let the mortifyingly empty card fall into its respective place. With her profession, Richard would, no doubt, see a fickle lady who'd carried a regard for the man he called friend for three long years. How to make him see that for their brief acquaintance, she'd been more alive, more herself than she'd ever been? In him, she'd found a person who embraced her knowledge and would never stifle her keen need to know. "Thank you," she whispered.

Dark emotion flared in his eyes, momentarily robbing her of breath and thought. These were the eyes that had the power to delve into a woman's soul and with his gaze this too-brief moment, she was that woman. He lowered his head so close his breath tickled her cheek and she fluttered her lashes.

"Miss Reed—?"

No! At the unexpected interruption, a string of unladylike curses that would have shocked the king's guard ran through her head as she and Richard turned as one. Lord Westfield stood there, his usual, affable, charming self. And she'd never been more unmoved.

He looked pointedly to her dance card. "Will you do me the honor of this set?"

From the corner of her eye, she looked to Richard. The harsh planes of his face were set in an inscrutable mask. Those hard lips, that had given her the first taste of passion, and set off this hungering for more in his arms, formed a hard line. "Of course," Gemma said with forced cheer and held her card out to the marquess who promptly scribbled—She yanked her gaze to his.

As though taking some distant cue from the marquess, the orchestra struck the chords for the next set. A quadrille.

She stretched her smile to the point of breaking as she allowed him to escort her onto the dance floor. She cast a quick, lingering look at Richard, willing him to see the truth she'd only herself just discovered. He stood, hands in his pockets, and rocked on the balls of his feet, eying her and Lord Westfield a long while, and then he strode away.

"Are you enjoying yourself this evening, Gemma?" he murmured as they completed the first steps of the dance.

"Indeed, my lord."

With his hand at the small of her back, he led her in a small circle, and then they were briefly parted. Gemma used the moment to search out Richard and a pang of disappointment went through her when finding him gone.

The natural steps of the quadrille brought her and the marquess together once more. "You perform the steps of the quadrille with remarkable flourish and grace." He was everything gracious and polite and flattering and, yet, how empty those compliments rolled from his tongue.

You matter more than the match you might make or the approval of Society. You matter because you are a woman so wholly different than any other.

She could not maintain this oppressive facade, even for the benefit of Polite Society. With every utterance, Lord Westfield's words stifled her breath and hopes. Is this what life with him would be if they married? Heart hammering wildly, Gemma came to a sudden and jarring stop that brought the other partners in their circle to a stumbling halt. "I…" Aware of the flurry of whispers from the dancers about them, the confusion in the marquess' eyes, Gemma dropped a curtsy. "Please, excuse me."

Then, she fled. Gemma moved with a stealth and speed her mother would have lamented and her brother would have applauded. Slipping between the crush of guests, she attracted curious stares before they registered it was merely Miss Reed, whom they'd never felt deserving of that regard. Gemma escaped the ballroom and then with her heart beating a frantic rhythm in time to her footsteps, she tore down the hall. She skidded to a halt outside the duke's library and fumbled with the door handle before managing to open it and slip inside. Some of the tension seeped from her heaving shoulders as she closed the panel behind her and leaned against it, taking support from the wood surface. She pressed her eyes closed and found a soothing comfort in the dull hum of silence that drowned out the peals of laughter and buzz of whispers she'd left behind.

Gemma took deep, steadying breaths and opened her eyes. She blinked. It took a moment to adjust to the darkened space. The thick scent of leather flooded her senses, calming and reassuring. How many years had she lost herself in the comfort of the pages of books? When she'd been friendless and battling the blunt, unkind honesty of first governesses and then the *ton*, she'd escaped within her quest for information and learning.

Now, with Richard having stolen into her life and heart, she could acknowledge the truth: how very lonely her life had truly been. None of those inked words could ever properly convey the depth of feeling to be had in—

The door opened and she went sprawling to the floor. Gemma landed hard on her knees with a loud grunt as pain shot up her legs. But through the pain was a thrilling charge of excitement. "R—" Her greeting died a quick death. Oh, God. Disappointment sank like a stone in her belly as the Marquess of Westfield quickly closed the door and rushed to her side.

"Gemma," he said with a familiarity that really should have existed for years given her friendship with Beatrice, but had only come to be during this week.

"M-My lord," she stammered, as he set her on her feet with a masculine ease. Except, the moment she was on her feet, the ticking long case clock in the opposite corner of the room punctuated the awkward pall between them. A thousand questions trailed through her mind as she fiddled with her skirts. Why was he here? Why...?

"I take it there is no surprise to you that my father has the expectation I will wed," he said suddenly with such casualness that she blinked several times.

For surely he'd not said..."My lord?" she blurted.

"Robert," he corrected. Then, he crossed over to the sideboard at the back wall. His hand hovered over the crystal decanters and then he froze mid-movement. "My father, I take it you know, is dying?"

There was an eerily haunting quality to the marquess' words; a dark emptiness that hinted at a man in pain, and as he spoke, it was as though he spoke to himself. But then, he shot a glance over his shoulder; his face a carefully expressionless mask.

"I am so sorry," she said gently, as some of the uncertainty around him lifted. Having lost her own father years earlier, she knew the pain of loss; particularly a beloved parent. She drifted closer and hovered at his shoulder.

He gave a terse nod and then returned his attention to the neatly arranged bottles. His Adam's apple bobbed, but then he gave his head a clearing shake and swiped the nearest decanter. "My father expects me to wed before..." The blood in his knuckles drained under the force of his grip upon his glass.

At his silent suffering, Gemma took another step closer. In times of grief and suffering, she'd come to appreciate that no words were needed. There was no need for ramblings or useless platitudes. Oftentimes, the assurance of another's presence, the truth that one wasn't alone in their misery, brought a soothing solace.

"Yes," he cleared his throat. "Well, he expects me to wed," he finished, neatly omitting the painful particular that had brought the lords and ladies together.

Distractedly, Gemma brushed her fingertips over the edge of the sideboard. "Isn't that the way of our world?" she asked softly. "They expect you to make a match even when sadness is sucking at your senses and stealing your thoughts."

He started, and at those honest words to escape her lips, she retreated a step. Lord Westfield, for even with his earlier offering, she could see him as no one but the marquess, continued to study her in a contemplative manner so that she shifted on her feet under that scrutiny. "It is expected I wed."

It was expected they all would wed. Granted, a nobleman who would be in possession of one of the oldest, most distinguished titles would be held to even more stringent expectations than a mere viscount's daughter.

Beatrice's brother, this man she'd long admired, propped his hip on the edge of the broad, mahogany piece and sipped from his glass of brandy. "If I marry, I would marry a woman I respect and admire. A woman who is loyal and trustworthy."

At having her own words, those ones she now saw as truly empty of all that mattered—love and passion…heat burned her neck. She cringed. What must Richard have thought when she made her confession to him earlier that week?

Lord Westfield took another swallow of his drink and then set the glass down with a soft thunk. "I admire and respect you, Gemma."

Gemma's world came to a jarring, screeching halt. For what did he truly know about her? Just as she'd known so very little about him. "Me?" she blurted. Oh, he was a devoted brother and a kind man. Time had proven that. But did he enjoy kippers or roast? Did he prefer hazard to faro? Or did he avoid those games of chance all together? The little pieces that made a person who they were, she couldn't even venture a guess, where the marquess was concerned.

The ghost of a smile played on his lips. "You are surprised."

Gemma smoothed her palms over the fabric of her skirts and picked around her thoughts for a suitable reply. After all, this moment was one that for three years she would have traded her left smallest finger for. Now, she gave thanks that no rash offering had been made or she'd be a finger short. Incapable of a suitable reply, she gave him none. He shot a hand out and brushed it along her cheek.

His touch, though sure and strong, was devoid of that jar full of electric energy. All the mad flutterings and tingles roused by Richard.

"Will you marry me?"

And after years of dreaming, there it was.

"Why?" she asked quietly.

The marquess swung the leg dangling from the sideboard back and forth, giving him an almost boyish quality. A small frown chased away his earlier smile. "We get along well enough." Well enough? They'd hardly spent any time together. "You are clever and I believe we'd have diverting conversations."

Despite herself, a smile tugged at the corners of her mouth. In the scheme of romantic marriage offerings, the marquess' would never be the manner of proposal that would find its way onto the pages of one of those shocking gothic novels or hopeful fairytales her mother enjoyed. Lord Westfield stared expectantly at her.

With the same careful attention she'd put to the lectures she attended in London and her books, Gemma contemplated that proposal. She had no doubt if she married the marquess they would have a degree of happiness together. They would be a content pair; perhaps one of those wedded couples that used one another's last name and title in discourse. A couple that would forever be subjected to Society's scrutiny until her every smile was weighted in falsity. There would be no grand passion but rather a gentle companionship and she wanted more. Things that would never be with this man, because another had set her heart aflutter.

"For three years, I have loved you to distraction, Lord Westfield," she said softly and that admission brought his swinging leg to an abrupt stop.

He flared his eyes, but otherwise gave no indication as to his thoughts to her revelation. Gemma held her palms up. "You danced with me when no one else would. You smiled at me and asked how I was doing, when others saw me as invisible." With a wistful smile, she wandered away from him and stopped along one of the floor-length bookshelves.

A horse book snagged her notice and she absently trailed her fingertips over the gold lettering etched on the spine of that tome. "I came here with the purpose of confessing my feelings to you." She directed those words to the book at her eye-level. Gemma shot a look over her shoulder. "I resolved to not let anything stop me from telling you everything I carried in my heart and arrived with the intention of doing so, and now I can." She turned her palms up once again. "Lord Westfield, for three years, I loved you."

He gave a tug at his previously immaculate cravat, saying nothing. She gave Lord Westfield a gentle, but understanding smile. This man would never be comfortable with admissions of love—at least, not from her. Because he did not love her. As Emery had said, the marquess had seen her for three years, but never truly saw her. Nor would he. And it was why she could easily reject the offer he put to her now.

Richard was a bloody coward. There was nothing else for it.

Because he was a glutton for self-torture, he'd stared blatantly at Gemma and Westfield performing the steps of a quadrille. The candle-light doused Gemma in a soft, shimmery glow, giving her an other-worldly beauty that marked her different than the sea of sameness that existed amongst the pallid ladies around her. His gut clenched. How had he ever believed her plain? How, when her eyes glittered with her every emotion; from tart-annoyance to unmitigated joy? A glow shined from those brown tresses that refused to curl, setting a lady already so wholly unique apart from the ladies lacking around her.

Now, with the image of Gemma in the arms of his closest friend res-onating inside the chambers of his mind, Richard slammed his empty flute down on the tray of a nearby servant. Careful to avoid any glimpse of the couples twirling upon that Italian marble floor, Richard strode along the length of the ballroom. He'd never been more grateful than when the pair parted ways and made off in opposite directions. Still, the memory of their pairing lingered and he hesitated. Unbidden, Richard searched her out, but found her gone.

She'd asked to meet him, but now, staring out at the smiling dance partners, his feet remained locked to the floor. *Mayhap you don't truly wish to know what the lady says? Mayhap because you know all she wants is to enlist your support to win Westfield's affection...?*

I need her to know. He fisted his hands hard as the truth slammed into him. Because if he did not at least confess that his heart belonged to her, then he would prove the same coward he'd always been.

With a silent curse, he took his leave, making his exit through the back door. In the course of his life, he'd demonstrated a shocking and deplorable tendency of running. First from Eloise. Then, *away* from Eloise when she'd married his brother. He'd not be that same coward where Gemma Reed was concerned, too.

As Richard turned the corridor, he slowed his steps. How long had he been running away from his unacknowledged, until now, insecurities that came from his birthright as second born son? For so long, he'd taken pride in his own accomplishments while secretly feeling an interloper in a world he'd been born to but, by rank, had only merited a place on the edge. With his footfalls muted by the thin carpet lining the corridor, he continued his forward path. As he walked, Richard looked at the stern-faced ancestors of the Somerset line peering down their ducal noses.

By rank and right, Westfield was deserving of Gemma Reed. For that matter, what lady in the whole of the kingdom would pass over a dukedom? Particularly a young lady who'd harbored a *tendre* for that same gentleman for years. A woman who'd spoken of love and her heart's desires.

He reached the library door and paused.

Yet, if he did not tell Gemma what was in his heart, if he did not tell her how she'd challenged him to look at everything he'd believed to be true for the course of his life, and then upended those unrealities in but five days, then it would be a regret that would dog him until he was a doddering gentleman with whitened hair and wrinkled hands.

Richard grabbed the door handle. When Gemma's voice sounded from the opposite side of the panel, he stayed his movements. He tried to make out her words but the wood panel muffled them. Richard's lips descended into a frown. Who in blazes was the lady meeting—?

"...Will you marry me?"

A dull humming filled Richard's ears. That voice he recognized. He recognized it because he'd been a friend of the man for more than twenty years. And hated himself for hating that same friend in this moment.

He'd offered for her.

Once again, in a trick of fate and time, Richard was too late. His stomach churned and he slid his eyes closed, an unwelcome and unwanted witness to this very private exchange. Yet, he could not force his legs away. Because he hung to the sliver of a fragile hope that she would say no. That Gemma had felt that same magnetic pull that had called to him from their first meeting in the woods. That Gemma would say no.

"For three years, I loved you…"

But she didn't say no. As her soft, lyrical voice reached his ears, Gemma gave Westfield every blasted word she'd intended, but erroneously given to Richard at her arrival five nights earlier.

Richard stilled and an unexpected pain scissored through him. It cut across his previous determined musings and left him standing there at sea. His hand fell to his side as he stood numb, staring at the door, staring as Gemma's previously quiet voice was strengthened with passion.

"…I resolved to not let anything stop me from telling you everything I carried in my heart…" He stood there, letting each word serve as a lash on his damned heart; a goddamn organ he'd thought incapable of this flood of emotions. "And I arrived with the intention of doing so, and now I can…"

A painful groan climbed up his chest and he took a step away from the door, and then another, and another, until his back knocked against the wall, rattling a painting with his careless movements.

Then, horror descended on his shoulders as he imagined Westfield opening that bloody door and finding Richard there, hovering outside. Mayhap, Westfield would invite him inside. Introduce him formally to his future duchess. Hands up, warding off the horrifying possibility, Richard tore down the hall as though the demons of hell were nipping at his heels.

And with the agony knifing at his heart, perhaps they were. With the distant din of the ballroom echoing in the corridors, Richard bypassed the inane amusements unfolding in that sweltering room and strode on to his guest chambers.

THIRTEEN

Odd how words had always escaped Gemma around the Marquess of Westfield and now, alone in his presence, with him putting an offer to her that any other lady present for this summer party would have sold her soul to the devil on Sunday for, it was so very easy to at last speak.

Gemma wandered over to the empty hearth and stared down at the cold metal grate. She'd never wanted the marquess. Not truly. Rather, she'd wanted the dream of what he'd represented. "For three years I convinced myself I loved you." She cast a sad smile over her shoulder, in his direction. "You were the greatest dream I'd carried in my heart for so long." The hope of him had sustained her through miserable ball after miserable ball. Only to now discover a young lady needing to find a reason to brave those lonely affairs had merely fabricated that dream. He'd given her that hope, for which she'd be forever grateful. But gratitude was no grounds with which to form a union.

The floorboards groaned, indicating he'd moved. "So why do I detect a rejection in your tone?" he murmured.

She turned, facing him squarely. "Because there is a rejection there," she said and then heat burned her cheeks. "A gentle rejection. A grateful one for your offer." His lips twitched and some of the tension left her on a sigh. "But yet, it is a no. Though I am grateful for your offer," she put in politely.

The marquess rolled his shoulders. "You are certain?"

She laughed softly. In all her grandest dreams of that magical moment of a gentleman asking for her hand, it had entailed beautiful words, promises of forever, and an avowal of undying love. Yes, for certain, romantic sentiments for a lady given to reason. That dream had never included a polite, if curt, "you are certain?"

"I am," she said, skimming her hand over the edge of the marble mantel. "But the truth is, I love another," she murmured, and then froze as the significance in sharing that admission with this man more stranger than she'd ever before conceded. Love filled her heart and the words tumbled out. "And he is all those things; good, loyal, kind, but more, he makes my heart race," Which the marquess had never done. "And I would be wrong to ignore the dictates of my own heart."

Silence met her pronouncement, which Lord Westfield broke. "He is a fortunate man."

He is your best friend. A spasm of pain contorted her face and she quickly dipped her gaze to the floor. For Richard would, no doubt, scoff at such a profession, particularly from a lady who'd days earlier attempted to give those words to Lord Westfield. "Perhaps," she said at last.

She stiffened as the marquess tipped her chin up with his knuckles. "No, perhaps. He is decidedly a lucky gent."

Gemma coughed into her hand, dislodging that touch. "Yes, well, it is a bit more complicated than that."

"Oh?"

How singularly interesting that the most ease they should know in any discourse between them these years should be from this intimate exchange that involved talks of the heart and offers of marriage. "I am afraid the gentleman is in love with another." There was, however, something cathartic in breathing the words into existence to this man who was not a loyal friend or devoted brother.

"Then he is a bloody fool and I'm sure he's not worth your affections. My offer still stands." He waggled his eyebrows and a laugh exploded from her lips. "That is better, Gemma."

The lady given to logic, she'd spent her life being wanted, stomped her foot. Why couldn't she love him? Why couldn't she love him and he love her? Then this entire exchange would be entirely different and it would result in happily-ever-afters and not this dull ache in her chest that felt not unlike the miserable infection she'd had as a girl of ten. "What if I were to say he is your friend?"

The marquess stared unblinkingly and then resumed a slow blink. "My...?" Then he widened his eyes. "*Jonas.*"

There were a million follies in why breathing that admission into existence was dangerous. A lady did not share matters of the heart with other gentlemen. There was the risk of discovery and ruin, and... "Richard Jonas," she said softly. But this man was Beatrice's brother and Richard's best friend. And even though he had no claim to Gemma's heart, for the kindness he'd shown her through the years, he'd proven himself a loyal friend in ways. "As such, I suspect you know he is, in fact, deserving, and..." she grimaced. "Very much in love with another."

Lord Westfield's eyes shuttered, concealing all hint of emotion but not before she detected the flash of regret and understanding. For there was Richard's Eloise and there would always be that paragon he'd exalted. Not unlike the way she'd raised Lord Westfield up as more than a mere mortal. Only Richard's love had been built on years of knowing and a bond forged in childhood. A vicious envy snaked through her, momentarily cutting off airflow. "What will you do?" he asked quietly.

"Tell him," she said unhesitatingly. What else could she do but share what was in her heart? Even if her feelings would not be returned. Even if he could promise her nothing because there would always be another, she was not so cowardly that she could not give him the words. Would not. Her gaze slid to the ormolu clock. "He will visit me here soon."

Understanding glinted in the marquess' eyes. "Ah, so this is why you are here."

She nodded once.

In one quick movement, Lord Westfield downed the contents of his glass and set it down on the mantel. "Well, then, I must leave you to your meeting. Wouldn't do to be discovered alone by Jonas, given the circumstances." He winked, raising another small laugh, which died when the marquess captured her fingers and brought her hand to his mouth.

"He is a good man, but you are decidedly a deserving woman." He dropped a kiss atop her hand and then with five long strides, crossed over to the door, opened it, and then left.

Gemma stared after him a long moment and then, fiddling with her skirts, claimed a spot on one of the leather winged back chairs at the hearth—and proceeded to wait.

"Jonas."

Richard could pretend he didn't hear that staying call. He could turn the corner of the hall and pretend he was so engrossed in his own thoughts and the distance between him and Westfield at the end of the hall so great, he'd failed to hear.

"Jonas," the other man boomed again.

This time, Richard stopped his forward stride. Alas, having been born and groomed early as a future duke, Westfield was one who'd learned early on that all stopped to notice him. It was not a thing to envy the man for, rather it was a matter of fact. Staring at the opposite wall, he allowed the other man to close the distance between them and, schooling his features into an indiscernible mask, forced himself to turn.

He braced for the transformative words that would further rip open his already battered heart; words indicating that he'd become betrothed.

"You are not attending the ball?"

And this is what the gentleman would say?

Furrowing his brow, he stared at Westfield. So long, in fact, that the man arched an eyebrow. He started. "I did attend the ball and I am now returning to my chambers."

"Your chambers?" the man pressed and folded his arms.

"I plan to ride out early on the morn. Is there somewhere else you'd expect me to be?" he growled.

Meet me in the library. That no longer necessary meeting where Richard would have given Gemma assistance in her quest for Westfield's hand. In the end, she'd never needed it. She never had.

"But…"

Richard eyed the man expectantly. *Do not say it. Do not mention your betrothal to Miss Gemma Reed and all the joyous festivities that would commence following that pronouncement.* "What is it?" He curled his fingers into tight balls.

"I just thought…" Westfield shook his head once. "I just thought you might have more of a reason to stay."

He did. It was, ironically, also the reason he had to leave.

Then, Richard had long excelled in running. With the exception of horse breeding, it was the one thing he'd done with a remarkable ease. His feet twitched with the need to make a midnight retreat. But when he'd arrived at the duke's country party, he'd promised to meet Westfield about acquiring a Friesian. His stomach muscles knotted. Richard would be forced to sit across from the other man and talk about a bloody mare for his sister, casually discussing business transactions and details about the mount when all the while Gemma remained the unspoken, but forever-divisive, wedge between them.

Westfield searched his gaze over his face. He looked as though he wished to say something but simply said, "You are certain you need to leave?"

"I do." At the reproachful look, a frisson of guilt went through him. When Richard had been invisible to the other boys at Eton because of his less than lofty status and his odd tendency to run on about everything horses, Westfield had been steadfast—in his friendship, in his loyalty. When Richard had mourned Eloise's marriage to first a powerful earl, and then later to Lucien, Westfield had kept company with his miserable self, allowing him to get soused. For that loyalty, Richard owed the other man *some* explanation. "There is other business I have to attend," he said quietly. After all, what more important chore was there than maintaining one's sanity?

"Ah, yes. *Business.*" When stated in that faintly disapproving way, it was as though the other man did, indeed, see. See that Richard was a miserable bastard who'd covet the lady his best friend would one day soon marry. "Before you depart for home, do you still intend to meet with me to discuss the mount for Beatrice?"

Richard swallowed down a black curse. There was a probing glint in the man's eyes. What was home, exactly? It was no longer the place he'd grown up as a boy, running through the hills with his brother and Eloise. It was not this place he'd found an equal comfort in during his earlier years.

It was a person. And that person would belong to another. Nay, she'd belong to Westfield. Jealousy, knifelike and jagged, slivered away at his insides, chipping away all warmth.

"Of course," he said tightly. "On the morn, then?" He sketched a bow and made to leave when Westfield held up a staying hand. Gritting his teeth, he forced his features into a smooth mask, braced again for that revelation that would knock Richard's feet out from under him.

"I understand you were hurt by Eloise's marriage to Lucien."

Eloise? Richard blinked slowly. Of all the words he'd expected, mention of Eloise had assuredly not been the ones. Gentlemen partook in drinks and overindulged in spirits to silently lament the breaking of a man's heart, they did not, however, speak candidly on it.

"You always deserved a lady who wanted only you. And I believe if you but look before you, you'll find that woman." Westfield cast a glance in the opposite direction he'd just traveled. The library.

I did. Bitterness crept into his thoughts.

"Eloise was never that woman," the other man said matter-of-factly. "In time, I expect you'll realize that." With that, Westfield took his leave.

I already have.

And as the marquess disappeared around the hall, Richard quietly entered his rooms and closed the door with a soft click. On wooden legs, he wandered over to the edge of the bed and sank onto the edge of the mattress. With a ragged groan, Richard buried his head in his hands—and damned the day Gemma Reed had stepped into his riding path.

FOURTEEN

He hadn't come.

With the hum of silence thunderous in her guest chambers, Gemma glared at the bedroom door.

Last evening, for the request she'd put to Richard and his pledge to come, he had never shown. She'd sat there so long thinking at first he'd been waylaid. And then when the minutes continued ticking by and turned over the first hour, she'd convinced herself that she'd forgotten to mention the specific room where he might find her. With that, she'd sat in guilt, imagining him opening door after countless door in the duke's palatial country estate.

And then somewhere when the sun had crept above the horizon a painfully bright crimson and red orb, she'd forced herself to acknowledge the truth.

Richard wasn't coming.

There had been no mistake or misunderstanding. There had been nothing more than a man who'd not cared as deeply as Gemma herself to even merit honoring that meeting.

For the better part of the morning, she'd been consumed with a nauseating sadness. Until she'd promptly rationalized her way through her reaction to find she'd only allowed herself to become one of those morose, pining ladies. One could say what one would about Gemma; ugly, odd, eccentric, but one would never dare call her a pining lady.

A knock sounded at the door and she welcomed the interruption. It provided a diversion from the tumult of emotion swirling in her chest. Gemma jumped to her feet and sailed across the room in a whir of noisy skirts and pulled the door open.

Beatrice froze mid-knock, unblinking like an owl.

"Beatrice."

The greeting sprung her friend into movement and she swept inside, closing the door shut with a firm click. Suspicion glinting in her eyes, her friend spoke without preamble. "You left the ball early last evening."

Of course, the same friend who'd loyally stood at her side through infernal gathering after gathering would notice Gemma's conspicuous absence. Her mind raced. "I developed a headache." Which wasn't entirely untrue. She'd been riddled with bothersome thoughts of a certain horse breeder since he'd broken his promise.

She recoiled as Beatrice leaned close and peered into her eyes. "And you were not at breakfast."

"I was not hungry." That was at least the truth.

The young lady said nothing for a while, but rather scrutinized Gemma until she shifted on her feet. Then…"My brother intends to ride to the lake this morning."

At one time, that information would have mattered. No longer. Gemma slid her gaze away. For the friendship between them, Beatrice deserved the truth. "I cannot marry your brother."

Her friend tipped her head. "But you love him," she blurted. Gemma opened her mouth to speak when the other young lady spoke in a flurry. "Oh, I understand he is a dunderhead most of the time who does not always see what is right before him." She began to pace a small path in front of Gemma. "He is hopelessly obstinate and not always romantic." The agitated pace sent a perfect, golden curl falling over her brow. "Oh, very well," she muttered and then blew at the strand. "Not at all romantic."

Gemma took her friend by the shoulders and stopped her frenetic movement. "Your brother will someday be romantic, but I suspect only with the lady who earns his heart." She gave her a gentle smile. "I however, am not that woman."

Beatrice's lips formed a small moue. She opened and closed her mouth several times and then said, "You do not love him." The same wonder of the astronomers who'd discovered the sun was, in fact, the center of the universe lined her words.

"I do not love him," she confirmed.

At that concession, Beatrice's shoulders sank. "But you were going to marry him and live happily ever after, and we were to have been sisters and—"

"And I do not need to wed Lord Westfield to call you sister." Gemma gave her shoulders a slight squeeze. Their friendship had been borne of a close bond of two ladies who both desired more—from life and love. Who Gemma wed had no bearing on that kindred connection.

A look passed between them and then some of the disappointment receded from her friend's eyes. "Very well," she said in a perfunctory manner. Then a grin turned her lips. "Who is the gentleman who's earned your heart?"

Of course, given that friendship, Beatrice would never be content with that telling and, yet, vague revelation. At the prolonged silence, four lines creased the other woman's brow. Gemma sighed and stepped away. "Richard...Mr. Jonas," she said at last.

Fluttering her hand to her lips, Beatrice covered her mouth with her palm. "*Mr.* Jonas?"

As Gemma did not quite know what to make of the consternation in that two-word inquiry, she wandered away, walking to the window. With restless fingers, she drew the curtain back and stared out at the cloud-less summer sky. Where was he even now? She did a sweep of the rolling green pastures, squinting off into the distance. She looked toward the invisible to the eye copse that marked that special place shared by she and Richard. "Mr. Jonas," she murmured, more to herself.

In the crystal windowpane, Beatrice slid into focus. "I did not know that you..." The young lady cleared her throat and then pressed ahead. "...*knew* Mr. Jonas."

Releasing the curtain, Gemma turned, and as Beatrice deserved the whole of it, she recounted all of her meetings with Richard. When she'd finished, a wistful smile danced on her friend's lips, because where Gemma had forever been the clear-headed one, Beatrice had been the romantic. Oh, Society did not know, nor suspect that the regal duke's daughter held onto the dream of love, but Gemma knew, and that whimsical trait was never more obvious in this moment.

Then, Beatrice's smile dipped. "He is leaving."

Of course their time here would end and by his failure to meet last night, the end had been signaled sooner than later. Still, even with that, pain squeezed like a vise about her heart. How dare he? How dare he enter her life and upend her world and leave without so much as a by your leave? Gemma curled her hands into hard fists and welcomed the comforting fury thrumming through her veins, the sentiment far safer than the gripping pain.

Beatrice touched her shoulder and Gemma stiffened. "I saw him riding earlier with his fishing equipment." The *ton* saw nothing more than a proper English lady in Beatrice. The actuality was, not unlike Gemma, she'd long perfected the art of escape from their notice.

She narrowed her eyes. Fishing equipment. He'd gone off *fishing?* The lout. "Did you?"

"He was alone." Those words hung meaningfully in the silence.

He was alone. That meant if Gemma was so inclined, she could seek him out. Where she'd sought him out yesterday evening for altogether different purposes, now her feet twitched with the urge to sprint off, find Richard, and…The fight drained from her body and out the soles of her slippers. And what? Berate him for not wanting her with the same desperate regard that she wanted him?

She dragged her palm over her forehead.

The other woman nodded.

Gemma wanted to send Richard to the devil for his perfidy, but more, she wanted to see him—and share everything she carried in her heart.

A slow smile spread on Beatrice's cheeks. "That is better. You may borrow one of my mounts."

"I do not require a mount," she graciously declined.

So it was, not for the first time since she'd arrived at the Duke of Somerset's house party, Gemma found herself slipping off without the benefit of a chaperone. The sun beat down on her neck, warming her face. She would return with reddened skin and a freckled nose and to a furious diatribe from her mother. Adjusting the burden in her arms, she made the same familiar trek across the duke's property, trudging along. However, braving her mother's wrath would, indeed, be worth this final exchange. With each step, the clean, summer air filled her lungs and she contemplated what she'd say to Richard Jonas. She gritted her teeth.

Never showed, had he? Ignored her request? Nay, pledged to meet, and never came. Where was the honor? Those were not the actions of the gentleman she'd come to love. And it only increased the healthy fury rolling through her.

Where anything as undignified as perspiring had been sternly forbidden, Gemma had welcomed the invigorating cleansing that came with exercise. It was purifying and had the power to blot out the muddied and muddled thoughts.

She reached the copse and came to a slow stop, only to be proven a liar, once again, in life. She wasn't calm and she wasn't composed. She was hurt and furious. Only, she had no right being upset with Richard for caring, nay, loving another. She hated herself for not having the ability to love someone who "saw her", as her brother had so aptly said.

All perceived attempt at equanimity and control lifted. Standing there, on the outside of Richard's sanctuary, her palms grew moist. She picked her way through the densely wooded area, scanning for a hint of him. And then came to a stop.

With a smooth, fluid movement, Richard cast his reel into the lake.

A sweat-dampened lock fell over her eye and she shoved it behind her ear. Oh, the lout. Only a man could be so composed as to fish when a woman stood embroiled in a maelstrom of emotion. Gemma withdrew an arrow and loaded her archer's bow. She let the arrow fly into the trunk of the tree beside Richard.

A curse escaped him and the pole slipped from his fingers and fell to the ground. In one fluid movement, he spun to face her.

"You, sir, are a liar." Her chest heaved from the force of her emotion.

"What did you say?" He looked at her through thick lashes. At his infuriating calm, she shifted her archery equipment over to her other arm and jabbed a finger in his direction.

"I. Said. You. Are. A. Bloody. Liar." Which wasn't quite true. After all, she'd merely called him a liar. With each word, she took a step closer. "You, Mr. Jonas, promised to meet me." He retreated a step. "You were not there." He continued backing up. "Do you know how long I waited for you?"

Richard gave his head a brusque shake.

"Until the sun came up, Mr. Jonas." With his heels at the back of the lake, she stopped, and stuck her finger in his chest. Then promptly winced. Must he have a chest made of sheer stone? It only added to her healthy anger. "I waited and you never came. You don't promise to meet a lady and then never show." She hated the faint quiver to her words, but hated more the softening in his eyes. "Nor do I want your pity."

"I do not pity you, Gemma." There was a gruff quality to his tone so very different than the smooth, modulated ones she'd come to expect in every other gentleman. It marked Richard real in ways none of those other foppish lords had ever been.

She shot her chin up. "Good, because I do not want it." Gemma sank back on her heels and ran an agonized gaze over his face. "Why did you not—?"

"Why are you here?" His quiet interruption cut into her inquiry.

"What?" she blurted, her diatribe dying a swift death.

"I didn't expect you to be here."

Emotion roiled in her chest. Where did he expect she'd be? Giggling and embroidering with the other ladies at the duke's estate? Surely, even with the short time he'd known her, he'd gathered that she was not like those other women.

Richard shifted, presenting his back to Gemma, and staring out at the smooth, glassy surface of the lake. "I understand congratulations are in order," he said into the silence.

"Congratulations?" she repeated dumbly. What was he on about?

"I…" he cleared his throat. "Arrived during your meeting with the marquess."

She opened and closed her mouth several times. "You overheard my meeting?" That revelation escaped her on a breathless exclamation. The gravel crunched under her boots as she took a step closer.

From over the collar of his shirt, color stained Richard's neck. "It was not my intention to listen to such a personal exchange," he said huskily.

Yet...he had. He'd stayed long enough so that he could hear her exchange with Robert. Gemma muddled through her thoughts. If he'd listened in on their meeting, he'd know even now that her heart only belonged to him. Her heart slowed. *Mayhap he heard and does not want your love. Mayhap, he is telling you indirectly that you belong with another because you can never belong to him...*"Did you by chance hear the whole of our meeting?" Where did she find the courage to put forth that question?

"I heard enough."

Her heart stopped. "You heard what I said, then." *Oh, God.* The bow quivered in her arms and she steadied her hold.

His expression grew shuttered. "I did." Just two words. Two syllables that made a mockery of the love she carried for him. She bit her lower lip hard enough to draw blood. How coolly unaffected he was. Did he know that with each casually spoken word, he ravaged her sanity? He started for his fishing equipment.

She stared unblinking, feeling much like an outside observer as Richard crouched beside the massive oak and proceeded to gather his belongings. That was all he'd say? With his careless, dismissive movements and silence stretching on, a seething regret and resentment built inside her. That she should love him so and he could carry on fishing and moving about his daily motions as though he'd not upended her world and stolen her heart.

Richard opened his pack and dropped his silver hooks inside.

Oh, she'd had quite enough. Gemma removed an arrow and shouldering her bow, she set an arrow sailing. It hissed in the morning stillness and again lodged in the tree just above his head.

He barked in surprise. Tumbling backwards, Richard landed on the muddied ground. "What in hell?" From where he sat, sprawled on his buttocks, his eyes blazed with shocked fury.

She'd gone and lost her heart to a gentleman so wholly unmoved, and *he* was the furious one? "*You* are angry?" Gemma sent another arrow sailing. Her second missile stuck in the earth just between his legs.

Richard's eyes flared so wide, his eyebrows reached his hairline. Mouth agape, he alternated his stare between the arrow so very close to his manhood and Gemma. "Are you mad, woman?"

"Yes." She gave her head a hard nod. "I am furious."

"I meant insane," he gritted out. With a growl, he motioned to her well-placed arrow. "Were you trying to unman me or kill me?"

"Neither," she snapped. "I assure you, I do not miss, Richard Jonas. If I'd wanted to kill or maim, you'd be wearing my arrow."

At her words, he narrowed his eyes, looking at her through thick, hooded lashes.

Gemma tossed aside her bow. "You'd simply leave without allowing me my meeting?" She detested the hurt tremble to those words. "You cared so little that you'd not allow me to tell you…" *What is in my heart.* She winced, as the echo of some of the earliest words she'd spoken to him, about another, echoed between them.

Richard searched his gaze over her face and in one fluid movement, shoved himself to his feet. "Gemma?"

She'd thought she could hate nothing more than the cool indifference in his previous words. She'd been wrong. This tender concern stuck in her heart. She swallowed hard. "I thought, given…what we'd shared," She winced. For what they'd shared had clearly meant more to her than him. Unable to meet the piercing intensity of his gray-eyed stare, she glanced down at her forgotten arrow. "I thought you'd at least come to me." Even as it wasn't his fault that he didn't love her, even though one couldn't help where one loved, as she'd learned at this man's hands, bitterness blended with regret and hurt, roiling inside in a violent maelstrom of emotion.

"You are right," he said gruffly and she shot her attention back to his face. The column of his throat worked. "I should have stayed…and congratulated you on your…" A pained grimace contorted his face. "…upcoming nuptials."

Her upcoming nuptials? What was he…? The world slowed to an infinite stop. She gasped and then the Earth resumed its rapid spinning.

Oh, God. He'd not heard the whole of the conversation. He'd heard but a part…Hope stirred in her breast. A gentle breeze rolled through the forest and rustled the branches overhead. She closed the distance between them, stopping at the edge of the shore, and touched a hand to Richard's arm. "Is that why you did not meet me?" she whispered. "*You* believed I'd professed my love to Lord Westfield."

He remained silent so long she believed he'd not answer. "Did you not?" he said between tight lips.

"Oh, Richard," she layered her palms to his chest. His heartbeat pounded under the weight of her palms.

A sound of protest rumbled in his chest. "Gemma." He pressed his eyes closed, his face contorting as though physically pained. "If we are discovered, you'll be ruined. Forced to marry me."

Gemma's chest tightened as though a vise were being tightened about her. Did he even now see those titled lords as superior? "Would that be the very worst thing?" she put in tentatively.

He gave his head a hard shake and opened his eyes. The emotion from within their fathomless depths seared her. "I'd not have you this way. Not like this. Not trapped and caught when your heart belongs to another. A worthy gentleman I call friend."

Oh, Richard. How could he still not see the weight of his worth was far greater than all the dukes, marquesses, and earls combined. "Look at me," Gemma urged with a firm insistence and he looked down at her. She shifted and the water lapped noisily, dampening the hem of her skirt. "If you had met me last night, you would have known that Lord Westfield offered me marriage." Pain glinted in his eyes, but he remained motionless. Silent. "You would also know that I declined his offer."

She'd declined Westfield's offer of marriage?

The tree branches rustled overhead and the leaves danced noisily. Through nature's soft sounds, Richard tried to sort through her words. He gave his head a shake. "I don't…"

"I said no," she repeated softly and claimed his hands.

Richard looked down at their interlocked fingers. "You said no?" he rasped. Why, when she'd longed for Westfield for three years? Faint hope stirred within his chest. A memory trickled in, of his meeting with that other man last evening.

You always deserved a lady who wanted only you and I believe if you but look before you, you'll find that woman...

The air left him on a hiss. He'd known. Westfield had known.

Gemma nodded. "I did." Emotion shadowed her eyes. Unrepentant and honest, as she'd been since the day she'd crashed into the billiard's room, stealing his quiet, his heart, and his every thought.

He struggled to formulate a coherent reply past his thickened throat. "Why?" Silently pleading for it to be him because where Gemma existed, he had no pride. Selfishly, he wanted her in every way at his side.

"You see, I could not accept his offer until I shared what was in my heart—with you."

"Gemma?" he urged.

With a soft smile, she squeezed his hands. "I would have you know the words I carry in my heart." Those words eerily similar to ones she'd uttered six days earlier, but yet entirely different for reasons that robbed him of thought, froze his movements and held him suspended. "Richard Jonas, I've loved you since you whispered in my ear about horse vomit." His lips pulled. "I loved you even more when you encouraged me to be no one other than myself and spoke as though I was a woman different than all others—"

"There is no one else like you," he said hoarsely. And there wasn't. She possessed a spirit and wit that had beckoned since the first day she'd stepped into his riding path, chattering about fishing and light.

"And a man who looks at me as though I'm beautiful," she continued.

"Because you are." Her beauty shone from the inside out and set her aglow with a rich vibrancy that not even Athena herself could rival.

She pressed her fingertips to his lips, stopping his words. "And as I love you, I thought you should know the feelings in my heart, even as I know your heart belongs to your El—"

Richard took her mouth under his in a silencing, questioning kiss. No one else: not Westfield, not Eloise had a place in this moment that belonged entirely to them. A shuddery sigh escaped Gemma's lips and as her body melted into his, he caught her against his chest to keep her from dissolving. He broke the kiss and touched his lips to her temple. "You forced me to see that what I felt for Eloise was not love." He paused, thinking of the vicious envy that had nearly destroyed him whenever he imagined Gemma in Westfield's arms.

Gemma ran a questioning gaze over his face. "It wasn't?" she asked with a hesitancy that flew in the face of the manner of woman she was.

"I loved the familiarity of her," he conceded. And he would be forever indebted to that woman for reuniting his once fractured family. But gratitude was not love. "I loved the comfortable presence of a person I'd known for the better part of my life, but I did not truly know her." He knew that now. Richard palmed her cheek and lashes fluttering, she leaned into his caress. "Gemma Reed, I have loved you since you spoke about a horse's teeth and gestational period," he whispered. A watery smile turned her lips. "And I loved you even more when you challenged Society's strictures and expectations for young ladies." Richard dropped his brow to hers. "Gemma Reed, *you* are my heart's greatest yearning and I would ask you to marry me."

Tears filled her eyes. "Richard Jonas, you used my declaration."

"That is hardly an answer, love." His heart tripped an uneasy rhythm and he managed a lopsided grin. "Will you—?"

She leaned up on tiptoe and pressed her lips to his. Honeysuckle wafted about his senses, more intoxicating than any spirit he'd consumed. Of their own volition, his hands settled at her waist and he dragged her into the vee between his legs. An agonized groan burst from his lips as she drew back.

"That is a yes, Richard Jonas. That is a yes."

The End

BIOGRAPHY

Christi Caldwell is the bestselling author of historical romance novels set in the Regency era. Christi blames Judith McNaught's "Whitney, My Love," for luring her into the world of historical romance. While sitting in her graduate school apartment at the University of Connecticut, Christi decided to set aside her notes and try her hand at writing romance. She believes the most perfect heroes and heroines have imperfections and rather enjoys tormenting them before crafting a well-deserved happily ever after!

When Christi isn't writing the stories of flawed heroes and heroines, she can be found in her Southern Connecticut home chasing around her feisty five-year-old son, and caring for twin princesses-in-training!

Visit www.christicaldwellauthor.com to learn more about what Christi is working on, or join her on Facebook at www.facebook.com/christicaldwellauthor, and Twitter @ChristiCaldwell

For first glimpse at covers, excerpts, and free bonus material, be sure to sign up for my monthly newsletter at http://bit.ly/1Ngqcfj! Each month one subscriber will win a $35 Amazon Gift Card!

OTHER BOOKS BY

CHRISTI CALDWELL

"To Trust a Rogue"
Book 8 in the *"Heart of a Duke"* Series by Christi Caldwell

A rogue
Marcus, the Viscount Wessex has carefully crafted the image of rogue
and charmer for polite Society. Under that façade, however, dwells
a man whose dreams were shattered almost eight years earlier by a
young lady who captured his heart, pledged her love, and then left
him, with nothing more than a curt note.

A widow
Eight years earlier, faced with no other choice, Mrs. Eleanor Collins,
fled London and the only man she ever loved, Marcus, Viscount
Wessex. She has now returned to serve as a companion for her elderly
aunt with a daughter in tow. Even though they're next door neighbors,
there is little reason for her to move in the same circles as Marcus, just
in case, she vows to avoid him, for he reminds her of all she lost when
she left.

Reunited
As their paths continue to cross, Marcus finds his desire for Eleanor
just as strong, but he learned long ago she's not to be trusted. He will

offer her a place in his bed, but not anything more. Only, Eleanor has no interest in this new, roguish man. The more time they spend together, the protective wall they've constructed to keep the other out, begin to break. With all the betrayals and secrets between them, Marcus has to open his heart again. And Eleanor must decide if it's ever safe to trust a rogue.

"To Wed His Christmas Lady"
Book 7 in the "Heart of a Duke" Series by Christi Caldwell

She's longing to be loved:

Lady Cara Falcot has only served one purpose to her loathsome father—to increase his power through a marriage to the future Duke of Billingsley. As such, she's built protective walls about her heart, and presents an icy facade to the world around her. Journeying home from her finishing school for the Christmas holidays, Cara's carriage is stranded during a winter storm. She's forced to tarry at a ramshackle inn, where she immediately antagonizes another patron—William.

He's avoiding his duty in favor of one last adventure:

William Hargrove, the Marquess of Grafton has wanted only one thing in life—to avoid the future match his parents would have him make to a cold, duke's daughter. He's returning home from a bliss-ful eight years of traveling the world to see to his responsibilities. But when a winter storm interrupts his trip and lands him at a falling-down inn, he's forced to share company with a commanding Lady Cara who initially reminds him exactly of the woman he so desperately wants to avoid.

A Christmas snowstorm ushers in the spirit of the season:

At the holiday time, these two people who despise each other due to first perceptions are offered renewed beginnings and fresh starts. As this gruff stranger breaks down the walls she's built about herself, Cara has to determine whether she can truly open her heart to trusting that any man is capable of good and that she herself is capable of love.

And William has to set aside all previous thoughts he's carried of the polished ladies like Cara, to be the man to show her that love.

"The Heart of a Scoundrel"
Book 6 in the "Heart of a Duke" Series by Christi Caldwell

Ruthless, wicked, and dark, the Marquess of Rutland rouses terror in the breast of ladies and nobleman alike. All Edmund wants in life is power. After he was publically humiliated by his one love Lady Margaret, he vowed vengeance, using Margaret's niece, as his pawn. Except, he's thwarted by another, more enticing target—Miss Phoebe Barrett.

Miss Phoebe Barrett knows precisely the shame she's been born to. Because her father is a shocking letch she's learned to form her own opinions on a person's worth. After a chance meeting with the Marquess of Rutland, she is captivated by the mysterious man. He, too, is a victim of society's scorn, but the more encounters she has with Edmund, the more she knows there is powerful depth and emotion to the jaded marquess.

The lady wreaks havoc on Edmund's plans for revenge and he finds he wants Phoebe, at all costs. As she's drawn into the darkness of his world, Phoebe risks being destroyed by Edmund's ruthlessness. And Phoebe who desires love at all costs, has to determine if she can ever truly trust the heart of a scoundrel.

"To Love a Lord"
Book 5 in the "Heart of a Duke" Series by Christi Caldwell

All she wants is security:

The last place finishing school instructor Mrs. Jane Munroe belongs, is in polite Society. Vowing to never wed, she's been scuttled around from post to post. Now she finds herself in the Marquess of Waverly's household. She's never met a nobleman she liked, and when she meets the pompous, arrogant marquess, she remembers why. But soon, she discovers Gabriel is unlike any gentleman she's ever known.

All he wants is a companion for his sister:

What Gabriel finds himself with instead, is a fiery spirited, bespectacled woman who entices him at every corner and challenges his age-old vow to never trust his heart to a woman. But…there is something suspicious about his sister's companion. And he is determined to find out just what it is.

All they need is each other:

As Gabriel and Jane confront the truth of their feelings, the lies and secrets between them begin to unravel. And Jane is left to decide whether or not it is ever truly safe to love a lord.

"Loved By a Duke"
Book 4 in the "Heart of a Duke" Series by Christi Caldwell

For ten years, Lady Daisy Meadows has been in love with Auric, the Duke of Crawford. Ever since his gallant rescue years earlier, Daisy knew she was destined to be his Duchess. Unfortunately, Auric sees her as his best friend's sister and nothing more. But perhaps, if she can manage to find the fabled heart of a duke pendant, she will win over the heart of her duke.

Auric, the Duke of Crawford enjoys Daisy's company. The last thing he is interested in however, is pursuing a romance with a woman he's known since she was in leading strings. This season, Daisy is turning up in the oddest places and he cannot help but notice that she is no longer a girl. But Auric wouldn't do something as foolhardy as to fall in love with Daisy. He couldn't. Not with the guilt he carries over his past sins…Not when he has no right to her heart…But perhaps, just perhaps, she can forgive the past and trust that he'd forever cherish her heart—but will she let him?

"The Love of a Rogue"
Book 3 in the "Heart of a Duke" Series by Christi Caldwell

Lady Imogen Moore hasn't had an easy time of it since she made her Come Out. With her betrothed, a powerful duke breaking it off to wed her sister, she's become the *tons* favorite piece of gossip. Never again wanting to experience the pain of a broken heart, she's resolved to make a match with a polite, respectable gentleman. The last thing she wants is another reckless rogue.

Lord Alex Edgerton has a problem. His brother, tired of Alex's carousing has charged him with chaperoning their remaining, unwed sister about *ton* events. Shopping? No, thank you. Attending the theatre? He'd rather be at Forbidden Pleasures with a scantily clad beauty upon his lap. The task of *chaperone* becomes even more of a bother when his sister drags along her dearest friend, Lady Imogen to social functions. The last thing he wants in his life is a young, innocent English miss.

Except, as Alex and Imogen are thrown together, passions flare and Alex comes to find he not only wants Imogen in his bed, but also in his heart. Yet now he must convince Imogen to risk all, on the heart of a rogue.

"More Than a Duke"
Book 2 in the "Heart of a Duke" Series by Christi Caldwell

Polite Society doesn't take Lady Anne Adamson seriously. However, Anne isn't just another pretty young miss. When she discovers her father betrayed her mother's love and her family descended into poverty, Anne comes up with a plan to marry a respectable, powerful, and honorable gentleman—a man nothing like her philandering father.

Armed with the heart of a duke pendant, fabled to land the wearer a duke's heart, she decides to enlist the aid of the notorious Harry,

6th Earl of Stanhope. A scoundrel with a scandalous past, he is the last gentleman she'd ever wed…however, his reputation marks him the perfect man to school her in the art of seduction so she might ensnare the illustrious Duke of Crawford.

Harry, the Earl of Stanhope is a jaded, cynical rogue who lives for his own pleasures. Having been thrown over by the only woman he ever loved so she could wed a duke, he's not at all surprised when Lady Anne approaches him with her scheme to capture another duke's affection. He's come to appreciate that all women are in fact greedy, title-grasping, self-indulgent creatures. And with Anne's history of grating on his every last nerve, she is the last woman he'd ever agree to school in the art of seduction. Only his friendship with the lady's sister compels him to help.

What begins as a pretend courtship, born of lessons on seduction, becomes something more leaving Anne to decide if she can give her heart to a reckless rogue, and Harry must decide if he's willing to again trust in a lady's love.

"For Love of the Duke"
First Full-Length Book in the "Heart of a Duke" Series by Christi Caldwell

After the tragic death of his wife, Jasper, the 8th Duke of Bainbridge buried himself away in the dark cold walls of his home, Castle Blackwood. When he's coaxed out of his self-imposed exile to attend the amusements of the Frost Fair, his life is irrevocably changed by his fateful meeting with Lady Katherine Adamson.

With her tight brown ringlets and silly white-ruffled gowns, Lady Katherine Adamson has found her dance card empty for two Seasons. After her father's passing, Katherine learned the unreliability of men, and is determined to depend on no one, except herself. Until she meets Jasper…

In a desperate bid to avoid a match arranged by her family, Katherine makes the Duke of Bainbridge a shocking proposition—one that he accepts.

Only, as Katherine begins to love Jasper, she finds the arrangement agreed upon is not enough. And Jasper is left to decide if protecting his heart is more important than fighting for Katherine's love.

"In Need of a Duke"
A Prequel Novella to "The Heart of a Duke" Series by Christi Caldwell

In Need of a Duke: (Author's Note: This is a prequel novella to "The Heart of a Duke" series by Christi Caldwell. It was originally available in "The Heart of a Duke" Collection and is now being published as an individual novella.

It features a new prologue and epilogue.

Years earlier, a gypsy woman passed to Lady Aldora Adamson and her friends a heart pendant that promised them each the heart of a duke.

Now, a young lady, with her family facing ruin and scandal, Lady Aldora doesn't have time for mythical stories about cheap baubles. She needs to save her sisters and brother by marrying a titled gentleman with wealth and power to his name. She sets her bespectacled sights upon the Marquess of St. James.

Turned out by his father after a tragic scandal, Lord Michael Knightly has grown into a powerful, but self-made man. With the whispers and stares that still follow him, he would rather be anywhere but London…

Until he meets Lady Aldora, a young woman who mistakes him for his brother, the Marquess of St. James. The connection between Aldora and Michael is immediate and as they come to know one another, Aldora's feelings for Michael war with her sisterly responsibilities. With her family's dire situation, a man of Michael's scandalous past will never do.

Ultimately, Aldora must choose between her responsibilities as a sister and her love for Michael.

"Once a Wallflower, At Last His Love"
Book 6 in the Scandalous Seasons Series

Responsible, practical Miss Hermione Rogers, has been crafting stories as the notorious Mr. Michael Michaelmas and selling them for a meager wage to support her siblings. The only real way to ensure her family's ruinous debts are paid, however, is to marry. Tall, thin, and plain, she has no expectation of success. In London for her first Season she seizes the chance to write the tale of a brooding duke. In her research, she finds Sebastian Fitzhugh, the 5th Duke of Mallen, who unfortunately is perfectly affable, charming, and so nicely…configured…he takes her breath away. He lacks all the character traits she needs for her story, but alas, any duke will have to do.

Sebastian Fitzhugh, the 5th Duke of Mallen has been deceived so many times during the high-stakes game of courtship, he's lost faith in Society women. Yet, after a chance encounter with Hermione, he finds himself intrigued. Not a woman he'd normally consider beautiful, the young lady's practical bent, her forthright nature and her tendency to turn up in the oddest places has his interests…roused. He'd like to trust her, he'd like to do a whole lot more with her too, but should he?

"A Marquess For Christmas"
Book 5 in the Scandalous Seasons Series

Lady Patrina Tidemore gave up on the ridiculous notion of true love after having her heart shattered and her trust destroyed by a black-hearted cad. Used as a pawn in a game of revenge against her brother, Patrina returns to London from a failed elopement with a tattered reputation and little hope for a respectable match. The only peace she finds is in her solitude on the cold winter days at Hyde Park. And even that is yanked from her by two little hellions who just happen to have a devastatingly handsome, but coldly aloof father, the Marquess of Beaufort. Something about the lord stirs the dreams she'd once carried for an honorable gentleman's love.

Weston Aldridge, the 4th Marquess of Beaufort was deceived and betrayed by his late wife. In her faithlessness, he's come to view women as self-serving, indulgent creatures. Except, after a series of chance encounters with Patrina, he comes to appreciate how uniquely different she is than all women he's ever known.

At the Christmastide season, a time of hope and new beginnings, Patrina and Weston, unexpectedly learn true love in one another. However, as Patrina's scandalous past threatens their future and the happiness of his children, they are both left to determine if love is enough.

"Always a Rogue, Forever Her Love"
Book 4 in the Scandalous Seasons Series

Miss Juliet Marshville is spitting mad. With one guardian missing, and the other singularly uninterested in her fate, she is at the mercy of her wastrel brother who loses her beloved childhood home to a man known as Sin. Determined to reclaim control of Rosecliff Cottage and her own fate, Juliet arranges a meeting with the notorious rogue and demands the return of her property.

Jonathan Tidemore, 5th Earl of Sinclair, known to the *ton* as Sin, is exceptionally lucky in life and at the gaming tables. He has just one problem. Well…four, really. His incorrigible sisters have driven off yet another governess. This time, however, his mother demands he find an appropriate replacement.

When Miss Juliet Marshville boldly demands the return of her precious cottage, he takes advantage of his sudden good fortune and puts an offer to her; turn his sisters into proper English ladies, and he'll return Rosecliff Cottage to Juliet's possession.

Jonathan comes to appreciate Juliet's spirit, courage, and clever wit, and decides to claim the fiery beauty as his mistress. Juliet, however, will be mistress for no man. Nor could she ever love a man who callously stole her home in a game of cards. As Jonathan begins to see Juliet as more than a spirited beauty to warm his bed, he realizes she could be a lady he could love the rest of his life, if only he can convince the proud Juliet that he's worthy of her hand and heart.

"Always Proper, Suddenly Scandalous"
Book 3 in the Scandalous Seasons Series

Geoffrey Winters, Viscount Redbrooke was not always the hard, unrelenting lord driven by propriety. After a tragic mistake, he resolved to honor his responsibility to the Redbrooke line and live a life, free of scandal. Knowing his duty is to wed a proper, respectable English miss, he selects Lady Beatrice Dennington, daughter of the Duke of Somerset, the perfect woman for him. Until he meets Miss Abigail Stone...

To distance herself from a personal scandal, Abigail Stone flees America to visit her uncle, the Duke of Somerset. Determined to never trust a man again, she is helplessly intrigued by the hard, too-proper Geoffrey. With his strict appreciation for decorum and order, he is nothing like the man' she's always dreamed of.

Abigail is everything Geoffrey does not need. She upends his carefully ordered world at every encounter. As they begin to care for one another, Abigail carefully guards the secret that resulted in her journey to England.

Only, if Geoffrey learns the truth about Abigail, he must decide which he holds most dear: his place in Society or Abigail's place in his heart.

"Never Courted, Suddenly Wed"
Book 2 in the Scandalous Seasons Series

Christopher Ansley, Earl of Waxham, has constructed a perfect image for the *ton*–the ladies love him and his company is desired by all. Only two people know the truth about Waxham's secret. Unfortunately, one of them is Miss Sophie Winters.

Sophie Winters has known Christopher since she was in leading strings. As children, they delighted in tormenting each other. Now at two and twenty, she still has a tendency to find herself in scrapes, and her marital prospects are slim.

When his father threatens to expose his shame to the *ton*, unless he weds Sophie for her dowry, Christopher concocts a plan to remain a bachelor. What he didn't plan on was falling in love with the lively, impetuous Sophie. As secrets are exposed, will Christopher's love be enough when she discovers his role in his father's scheme?

"Forever Betrothed, Never the Bride"
Book 1 in the Scandalous Seasons Series

Hopeless romantic Lady Emmaline Fitzhugh is tired of sitting with the wallflowers, waiting for her betrothed to come to his senses and marry her. When Emmaline reads one too many reports of his scandalous liaisons in the gossip rags, she takes matters into her own hands.

War-torn veteran Lord Drake devotes himself to forgetting his days on the Peninsula through an endless round of meaningless associations. He no longer wants to feel anything, but Lady Emmaline is making it hard to maintain a state of numbness. With her zest for life, she awakens his passion and desire for love.

The one woman Drake has spent the better part of his life avoiding is now the only woman he needs, but he is no longer a man worthy of his Emmaline. It is up to her to show him the healing power of love.

"A Season of Hope"
A Danby Novella

Five years ago when her love, Marcus Wheatley, failed to return from fighting Napoleon's forces, Lady Olivia Foster buried her heart. Unable to betray Marcus's memory, Olivia has gone out of her way to run off prospective suitors. At three and twenty she considers herself firmly on the shelf. Her father, however, disagrees and accepts an offer for Olivia's hand in marriage. Yet it's Christmas, when anything can happen…

Olivia receives a well-timed summons from her grandfather, the Duke of Danby, and eagerly embraces the reprieve from her betrothal.

Only, when Olivia arrives at Danby Castle she realizes the Christmas season represents hope, second chances, and even miracles.

"Winning a Lady's Heart"
A Danby Novella

Author's Note: This is a novella that was originally available in A Summons From The Castle (The Regency Christmas Summons Collection). It is being published as an individual novella.

For Lady Alexandra, being the source of a cold, calculated wager is bad enough…but when it is waged by Nathaniel Michael Winters, 5th Earl of Pembroke, the man she's in love with, it results in a broken heart, the scandal of the season, and a summons from her grandfather – the Duke of Danby.

To escape Society's gossip, she hurries to her meeting with the duke, determined to put memories of the earl far behind. Except the duke has other plans for Alexandra…plans which include the 5th Earl of Pembroke!

"Tempted by a Lady's Smile"
Book 4 in the "Lords of Honor" Series

Richard Jonas has loved but one woman—a woman who belongs to his brother. Refusing to suffer any longer, he evades his family in order to barricade his heart from unrequited love. While attending a friend's summer party, Richard's approach to love is changed after sharing a passionate and life-altering kiss with a vibrant and mysterious woman. Believing he was incapable of loving again, Richard finds himself tempted by a young lady determined to marry his best friend.

Gemma Reed has not been treated kindly by the *ton*. Often disregarded for her appearance and interests unlike those of a proper lady, Gemma heads to house party to win the heart of Lord Westfield, the man she's loved for years. But her plan is set off course by the tempting and intriguing, Richard Jonas.

A chance meeting creates a new path for Richard and Gemma to forage—but can two people, scorned and shunned by those they've loved from afar, let down their guards to find true happiness?

"Rescued By a Lady's Love"
Book 3 in the "Lords of Honor" Series

Destitute and determined to finally be free of any man's shackles, Lily Benedict sets out to salvage her honor. With no choice but to commit a crime that will save her from her past, she enters the home of the recluse, Derek Winters, the new Duke of Blackthorne. But entering the "Beast of Blackthorne's" lair proves more threatening than she ever imagined.

With half a face and a mangled leg, Derek—once rugged and charming—only exists within the confines of his home. Shunned by society, Derek is leery of the hauntingly beautiful Lily Benedict. As time passes, she slips past his defenses, reminding him how to live again. But when Lily's sordid past comes back, threatening her life, it's up to Derek to find the strength to become the hero he once was. Can they overcome the darkness of their sins to find a life of love and redemption?

"Captivated by a Lady's Charm"
Book 2 in the "Lords of Honor" Series

In need of a wife…
Christian Villiers, the Marquess of St. Cyr, despises the role he's been cast into as fortune hunter but requires the funds to keep his marquisate solvent. Yet, the sins of his past cloud his future, preventing him from seeing beyond his fateful actions at the Battle of Toulouse. For he knows inevitably it will catch up with him, and everyone will remember his actions on the battlefield that cost so many so much—particularly his best friend.

In want of a husband…
Lady Prudence Tidemore's life is plagued by familial scandals, which makes her own marital prospects rather grim. Surely there is one gentleman of the ton who can look past her family and see just her and all she has to offer?

When Prudence runs into Christian on a London street, the charming, roguish gentleman immediately captures her attention. But then a chance meeting becomes a waltz, and now…

A Perfect Match…

All she must do is convince Christian to forget the cold requirements he has for his future marchioness. But the demons in his past prevent him from turning himself over to love. One thing is certain—Prudence wants the marquess and is determined to have him in her life, now and forever. It's just a matter of convincing Christian he wants the same.

"Seduced By a Lady's Heart"
Book 1 in the "Lords of Honor" Series

You met Lieutenant Lucien Jones in "Forever Betrothed, Never the Bride" when he was a broken soldier returned from fighting Boney's forces. This is his story of triumph and happily-ever-after!

Lieutenant Lucien Jones, son of a viscount, returned from war, to find his wife and child dead. Blaming his father for the commission that sent him off to fight Boney's forces, he was content to languish at London Hospital…until offered employment on the Marquess of Drake's staff. Through his position, Lucien found purpose in life and is content to keep his past buried.

Lady Eloise Yardley has loved Lucien since they were children. Having long ago given up on the dream of him, she married another. Years later, she is a young, lonely widow who does not fit in with the ton. When Lucien's family enlists her aid to reunite father and son, she leaps at the opportunity to not only aid her former friend, but to also escape London.

Lucien doesn't know what scheme Eloise has concocted, but knowing her as he does, when she pays a visit to his employer, he knows she's up to something. The last thing he wants is the temptation that this new, older, mature Eloise presents; a tantalizing reminder of happier times and peace.

Yet Eloise is determined to win Lucien's love once and for all...if only Lucien can set aside the pain of his past and risk all on a lady's heart.

"My Lady of Deception"
Book 1 in the "Brethren of the Lords" Series

***This dark, sweeping Regency novel was previously only offered as part of the limited edition box sets: "From the Ballroom and Beyond", "Romancing the Rogue", and "Dark Deceptions". Now, available for the first time on its own, is "My Lady of Deception".

Everybody has a secret. Some are more dangerous than others.

For Georgina Wilcox, only child of the notorious traitor known as "The Fox", there are too many secrets to count. However, after her interference results in great tragedy, she resolves to never help another...until she meets Adam Markham.

Lord Adam Markham is captured by The Fox. Imprisoned, Adam loses everything he holds dear. As his days in captivity grow, he finds himself fascinated by the young maid, Georgina, who cares for him.

When the carefully crafted lies she's built between them begin to crumble, Georgina realizes she will do anything to prove her love and loyalty to Adam—even it means at the expense of her own life.

NON-FICTION WORKS BY

CHRISTI CALDWELL

*Uninterrupted Joy: Memoir: My Journey through
Infertility, Pregnancy, and Special Needs*

The following journey was never intended for publication. It was written from a mother, to her unborn child. The words detailed her struggle through infertility and the joy of finally being pregnant. A stunning revelation at her son's birth opened a world of both fear and discovery. This is the story of one mother's love and hope and...her quest for uninterrupted joy.

Made in the USA
Columbia, SC
23 July 2020